THE JEWELS OF TERROR

As Frank Murray lay on his deathbed, he made one last wish: that his death not interrupt the plans for his daughter's marriage. And beautiful Veronica would not disobey.

But, as the wedding date grew nearer, eerie forces began to taunt and threaten Veronica, making it clear that there was someone who did not want her to marry, someone who would stop at nothing to destroy her life.

Soon, it seemed that her father's wish for a happy future had actually been a curse —damning her to the deepest and most frightening corner of hell...

THE JEWELS OF TERROR

The Jewels Of Terror

by
Janet Louise Roberts

MAGNA PRINT BOOKS
Long Preston, North Yorkshire,
England.

British Library Cataloguing in Publication Data.

Roberts, Janet Louise   *1925—*
   The jewels of terror.
   I. Title
   813.54 (F)

ISBN 0-7505-0011-5
ISBN 0-7505-0012-3 pbk

First Published in Great Britain by Severn House Publishers
Ltd., 1988

Copyright © 1970 by Script Associates, Inc.

Published in Large Print 1991 by arrangement with Severn
House Publishers Ltd., London.

Printed and bound in Great Britain by
Redwood Press Limited, Melksham, Wiltshire.

CHAPTER 1

Veronica smoothed the full skirts of the rose muslin dress and settled the white three-inch lace collar about her shoulders. Tiny white stars were embroidered over the muslin. Her white satin shoes peeped under the edge of the gown.

Her maid fastened the demure pearl necklace about her bare throat. Pearls were all the rage now in the 1890's. The woman set Veronica's blonde curls carefully in long rolls over her shoulders.

'This haste is indecent!' Sybil repeated angrily. Her black silk skirts rustled as she strode about the large bedroom. 'Your father scarcely dead a month! You aren't even wearing black for him!'

'Father hated black,' said Veronica softly. 'And he wanted me to marry Pietro. He had arranged the marriage himself. He put off the engagement party because he was dying.' Her throat closed on the words. Her small fingers rubbed the smooth neck. Her maid Jennie glanced at her, their eyes met in the mirror before the woman discreetly lowered hers.

7

'Disgraceful,' Sybil muttered, her face deeply flushed. The afternoon heat of the early September day had penetrated into the usually cool bedroom in the back of the stone and marble mansion of the Murray family, near Central Park in New York City. 'I want you to stay with me. I shall be so lonely now. Wait a little while. You could wait at least a year. Pietro would understand. He is a duke, after all.'

Veronica smiled, faintly, adjusted her lace gloves. 'Yes, and a very attractive Italian duke. All the best families are marrying their girls to European royalty. If I wait a year, another girl might snatch him!'

'It is not humorous, Veronica!' her stepmother snapped. Her green eyes flared with anger. 'I can see there is nothing to be gained by discussing this with you! I'll speak to Pietro! He is a gentleman. He understands etiquette.'

Veronica whirled around, her skirts flaring about her. She felt taller than her small five feet two as she turned on her stepmother. 'You will not speak to Pietro about this. We have settled the matter. Our engagement party is today, and we shall be married September twenty-third, just as father arranged!'

Sybil seemed to shrink before her unexpected fury. She stared incredulously at her quiet,

8

usually obedient stepdaughter. 'Your father spoiled you. No girl of mine would dare speak in that tone to me!' She turned and stalked out of the room, her back stiff.

After the door closed, Jennie whispered, 'Miss Veronica, you really should think. You don't know this Eye-talian duke fellow.'

'Father knew him, trusted him,' said Veronica. Her nerves felt tight to breaking, like a violin tuned too fine. Her mouth twisted. 'I must, I must get away...' she murmured.

She was thinking of the strange events of this past year, how her father had faded and died. He seemed to be eaten by something that consumed him, drained his strength. When he could no longer go to the designer studio, she had taken the plans and memos to Murray's Jewellery, and had seen that his wishes were carried out. He had leaned more and more heavily on her.

At the last, he had whispered to her, from the wide bed in which he seemed a shrunken skeleton, 'Darling...don't trust...I'm afraid... Sorry...terribly sorry... Go ahead with your wedding... *Pietro will protect you.*' He had hissed those words, with all his feeble strength, his face contorted in the effort to speak.

She had bent closer, desperately trying to make out his last words to her, straining to read

9

his lips, to understand what he was saying.

'Carry on...the business...you have...the talent...dearest Veronica...*be careful.*'

She had nodded, reassured him, patted his frail hands, so helpless on the covers, and he had lain back, panting.

'Careful,' she whispered now, as she went down the wide stairway, toward the back of the house to the gardens, to greet her guests with her future husband. 'Careful...of what? Of whom?'

Her skirts rustled as she swept through the downstairs hallway to the back living room, nearest the gardens. As she entered the room she saw Pietro Cavalcanti standing near the doorway, his face shadowed. His uncle and cousin stood near him. As she approached she heard them speaking rapidly in Italian.

She caught a few words, translated them. The fact that she had been taking private lessons in Italian for two years was a surprise for her future husband.

'Trouble. Pietro, think again. There is always Regina. You don't have to marry this foolish little American, and be attached to that dreadful nagging stepmother.' It was Giorgio saying the words.

She paused, her pulse seeming to stop for an agonizing moment. His relatives didn't want

10

this wedding either. And who was Regina?

'No. I won't break my word. I promised...' Pietro turned, saw her, forced a smile. He strode toward her, his dark brown eyes betraying a nervousness, an agitation. His long brown hand reached for her small cold one. 'Veronica, how lovely you look. Thank you for not wearing black.'

'Sybil was just scolding me,' she said tonelessly. 'She said we were rushing things. She wants me to stay with her for several months, help her recover from the shock of father's death.'

His mouth set in hard lines. 'No, that is not right,' he said crisply, his accent strong as it was when he was angry or deeply moved. 'The date has been set for months. Your father wished this. I am sorry for Mrs Murray. However, she must manage without you.'

His uncle Teodosio Cavalcanti moved away toward the garden, his silver head disdainfully high. Cousin Giorgio lingered, frankly listening, a slight mocking smile stirring his mouth as his dark eyes flickered over Veronica. The girl turned from him to gaze directly up at her fiancé.

'And you, Pietro,' she whispered urgently. 'Do you wish this wedding? Because if you don't we should not go ahead...'

His fingers touched her lips lightly, stopping the words. He gazed down at her, his eyes softening, his lean hard face more gentle. 'Yes, I wish it, cara. What does the world matter? This is between us. Yes?'

'Yes,' she said, and squeezed his hand in relief. 'All right. We'll go out there and announce our engagement ourselves. Sybil says she will not. She disapproves too much.'

He frowned. 'I will have my uncle to announce it then. That will be proper, as the next male relative. You have no other relatives, you said.'

'That is right. No one else...' She choked on the words, and held onto his hand as they went out into the bright sunlit garden. She had felt so desperately lonely and afraid since her father's death. There was no one, no one but Pietro, the stranger she was about to marry.

And there was still the mystery of her father's death. He had been only 48. Did a young vigorous man, happy in his work and in his family, wealthy, busy, begin to fade and die for no reason? Dr Heinrich had said so, he had found no other cause for death. Veronica could not believe it.

Frank Murray had left his estate and the family jewellery busines to his only daughter. Sybil, his second wife, was to receive a flat annual amount. Sybil had been stirred to anger. She had sworn the will had been altered and it had taken all three of her father's lawyers to persuade Sybil to accept the fact. She had finally calmed down to her usual cool self, and said that she realized Frank Murray had not considered her capable of managing the business.

Next May, when Veronica was 21, she would come into full possession of all her father's wealth. Until then, it would remain in trust. She was to direct the jewellery business, hire and fire, oversee both the New York Office and the Italian branch in Florence, which was headed by Pietro.

It was sensible also to marry Pietro, thought Veronica, as she walked beside him to greet their curious guests. She smiled, automatically, acknowledging their best wishes. Uncle Teodosio had made the announcement graciously, with regal dignity, in spite of the short notice Pietro had given him. She was marrying into a capable family, she thought. Pietro ran the Florence branch beautifully, and had done so for five years.

It was a merger of business and family as well as a marriage, she decided. The only trouble was, she didn't know how Pietro felt about her and the marriage—or how she herself felt.

A movement caught at the corner of her eye.

13

She turned her head and went cold. Sybil and Dr Heinrich were standing in a shadow, staring at her. Suddenly in the bright sunlight, with the scent of red roses filling the air, Veronica shuddered with a chill of fear. The tall blonde woman in black silk, her father's widow, was talking earnestly to the strange curt doctor who had attended her father in his fatal illness. The man was frowning at Veronica his black eyes gazing with rude intensity.

The shadow of an unknown fear, a chill warning gripped her. Her mind flickered over the possibilities, refused to accept them, rejected the possible evil. It could not be, it could not.

Pietro held her arm more closely to his body. 'Are you cold, cara?' he whispered. 'I will send for a cape, a scarf...'

'No, no, I'm all right.' She did like Pietro even if she did not know him well enough to love him. He was tall, handsome, intelligent, dignified, and had been a close friend of her father. The fact that he ran the Florence branch would be a great help to her in learning the business. She would have to run that branch and the New York office, somehow. Even though she was only a girl, her father had trusted her to carry on the business.

And she was desperate to get away from the darkness that had settled over the Murray

14

mansion with the death of her father. If she did not get away from her fears... She shivered again, so strongly that Pietro sent at once for a cape for her, and insisted on putting it around her shoulders. His tender anxiety helped soothe her fears.

They would marry. She would leave New York City and the nightmares she had here. She would live with Pietro in his beautiful villa near Florence. Villa d'Oro—the villa of gold, the golden house, she thought longingly. It sounded so sunny and beautiful and happy. Pietro had described it so she could practically see it, shining among the dark cypresses, set in its green emerald lawns like a topaz in its brooch.

'Veronica, darling!' A smooth cool hand caught her free hand. She looked up to blonde hair, greenish-grey eyes and a sweet smile.

'Diana! Oh, Diana!' The girls embraced impulsively. 'I thought you could not come! Oh, I'm so pleased to see you! Pietro, this is a dear friend from the convent school. Diana Jansson, my fiancé, Pietro Cavalcanti.' Veronica drew back from the tall girl's embrace, to glance up at her fiancé.

He smiled, more warmly than he had at her other friends. 'But we have met before,' he began, in pleased surprise, holding out his hand to Diana.

Diana clasped it, smiling at them both like a tall goddess bestowing blessings. 'Of course, at the fantastic ball last spring. So you are the man who captured my darling friend, Veronica! My best wishes to you both!'

Veronica felt the ice melting from around her as she chatted eagerly with her school friend, Pietro listened with a smile as they gossiped.

'And Julie, did you hear about Julie?'

'Oh, yes, she has a baby,' said Veronica, and then blushed deeply. Perhaps next year, this time, she too might have a child. 'And Susan is teaching in a school for Indians.'

'And Millie is working in the slums. Did you ever hear what Jeannette did?'

'But you, Diana. I thought you had gone out West!'

'I did, but just to get my dear aunt. She is to be my chaperon on a trip to Europe. Darlings, she is deaf,' she warned quickly, then caught the arm of a plump woman dressed in grey. 'Aunt Emily!' she screamed in her ear. Diana picked up the ear trumpet and put it to her aunt's ear. The face flickered with slight animation. 'This is Veronica Murray! And her fiancé, Pietro Cavalcanti!' Diana yelled. 'Aunt Emily Jansson!'

The woman nodded her grey fuzzy head,

said, 'So pleased to meet you,' in the low monotone of a person deaf for many years. 'Pretty girl!' she yelled unexpectedly at Diana.

Veronica giggled, felt Pietro shake briefly with mirth. Diana sighed, raised her greenish-grey eyes heavenward for a moment. 'A perfect chaperon, a deaf aunt,' she said, with mischief at the corners of her large red mouth. 'We're going to Naples, then to Rome for several months. I'm planning to paint seriously.'

'Oh, that is marvellous,' said Veronica, slightly surprised. Her vivid memories of Diana were as a daring leader of frolics, the girl who stayed out all night on a five-dollar bet, the girl who had defied the nuns till they had threatened to expel her. Diana had certainly matured. She had had some talent for art, but had not exhibited much interest in the intensive cultivation of her talents.

Other guests came up, and she and Pietro talked, listened, smiled, till they were weary. Finally the relatives and friends began to drift away. Giorgio and Teodosio went back to their hotel. Sybil left with Dr Heinrich, to Veronica's relief. Dusk began to settle over the roses in the garden, the sun had gone behind a cloud.

Diana waved a friendly farewell from the garden gate. How striking she was, thought Veronica, waving to her as she escorted her aunt out the gate. So tall, so beautiful in that stunning blue gown, so talented. Perhaps she would come to Florence to visit them.

'Pietro, I think we can go inside now,' she said.

'Good. I should like some coffee,' he said with a sigh and a twinkle. 'How exhausting engagement parties are! Let us never have another. Agreed?'

'Agreed!' she said and laughed with him. 'We can have our coffee in the drawing room. Perkins will light a fire, and we can sit and not talk at all if we choose!'

'My throat is weary, and so is my brain from talking English all afternoon.' said Pietro, thoughtfully. 'This gives me some conception of how it will be for you, darling, in Italy. You will tire of listening to us speak Italian. I have been thinking of some Italian lessons for you.'

Again she was about to confess that she had been taking lessons. Perkins approached her in the hallway, moving more rapidly than usual.

'Yes, Perkins?' she asked impatiently. She had just begun to talk in a more intimate manner with Pietro, and she hated to be interrupted.

'Mr Andrew Kelly is here, Miss Veronica. He insisted on speaking with you. I'm sorry, ma'am.'

'Show him into the drawing room. And bring coffee for all of us,' she said impulsively. 'Pietro, you don't mind, do you? Andy is probably here on business.'

His face had shadowed, but he shook his head. 'Of course. Do what you wish.'

They went into the drawing room. Perkins showed Andrew Kelly into the room soon after they had arrived. Perkins lit the fire in the fireplace as they greeted each other.

'I have just returned from Italy,' said Andy. 'My ship was late. I'm so terribly sorry!' He caught one of her hands warmly in both of his big ones.

She stared at the tall blond-haired man, the husky build and the blue eyes. Sorry about her engagement? Then she realized what he meant.

'My father, yes. It wasn't exactly sudden. He had been going down this past year, losing strength.'

'I realized he wasn't well. But the shock of hearing about his death was terrible. He was such a good man, so brilliant in his work. I had hoped to learn much more from him. But that is selfish of me—Veronica, please accept my heartfelt sympathy. If there is anything at all I can do, anything, ever, you must call upon me. I would consider it an honour.'

She clasped his hand tightly, then realized

19

they had been standing there holding hands under her fiancé's glare. She pulled her hand free.

'You are very kind, Andy. I don't believe you have met my fiancé, Pietro Cavalcanti. Andrew Kelly, one of the Murray designers, and a fine one. You will come to know him better soon, I am sure.'

Andy seemed to be somewhat shocked. He stared, finally held out his hand. Pietro accepted it with some reserve, his eyes dark and withdrawn.

Nervously, she asked them to sit down. Something had made the men bristle at each other like strange dogs. What in the world was wrong, she wondered. Andy was a fine artist. Her father had been lucky to get him. His father was one of the lawyers taking care of her father's estate, that had been the way her father had learned of Andy's talent, and had interviewed him. He had joined the firm a year and a half ago.

Andy practically turned his back on Pietro and told about his Italian journeys to Veronica. 'The Florence branch is doing well, with their selling, but I'm afraid the designs are old-fashioned. You know the new style is flowery and light and simple, rather than heavy and solid. I was hoping to present some new designs to your father...' He leaned forward on the couch, his face close to hers, his blue eyes searching her face eagerly.

She interrupted, embarrassed. 'I don't believe you understand, Andy. My fiancé is head of the Florence branch.'

Pietro was scowling, flushed. Andy flushed also as he realized his blunder. 'No, no, I hadn't—Cavalcanti—of course! I'm sorry. But it is true,' he stumbled onward bravely, with more courage than sense. 'The styles have changed, and Florence hasn't changed yet. We must do something, or the sales will drop sharply, and the imports go down.'

'That is exactly what I have been studying here in New York City,' said Pietro, sharply, his accent so heavy his words were blurred. 'Do you thing I have spent all my time here in being engaged to Veronica and attending parties? I work!'

'Of course, I understand,' said Andy, coldly disapproving.

'We are going to be married on the twenty-third,' Veronica interrupted the incipient quarrel. 'Then we sail for Italy. I'll be glad to see your reports before you go, and study the designs.'

They discussed that briefly, while Pietro drank his coffee, and refused sandwiches and cookies. She had a tight tense feeling, but didn't quite know what to do about it. Andy's eyes looked hurt, intense, puzzled as he looked from one to the other.

'Then, we'll meet at the office next Tuesday,' she settled the matter briskly. 'I'll go over your designs. You know, it would be helpful if you visited Italy this winter while I am there, and you could bring some new ideas, we could plan...'

'Fine! I hurried back before I had finished my plans for the Florence branch,' said Andy. 'Maybe I should come sooner.'

'Why don't you come about October? That would give you time to study, and then you could consult...'

Then she saw her fiancé's face. He was angry, his eyes blazing. Andy seemed to ignore Pietro deliberately, and went blithely on with his travel plans.

Andy finally left. A silence settled on the engaged couple. Veronica finished her coffee and offered more to Pietro rather timidly. He shook his head.

'I must leave at once,' he said. 'My uncle is expecting me this evening. Tomorrow I go to Boston on business.' He stood up.

She stood up also. He looked down at her, his eyes frowning as though he pondered what

22

he was going to say.

'Veronica, I must warn you about something,' he said, finally. 'In Italy, things are somewhat different. The women are not so free and easy with other men, only with relatives.'

'Free and easy!' she cried, outraged. 'I have never been so described!'

'American women,' he said, flatly, 'are much more friendly and unrestrained in their speech and actions. This will not be understood in Italy. I beg of you to consider carefully any actions that might cause gossip.'

'Pietro! I would never, never do anything that would cause gossip! You don't understand me! My father wanted me to carry on his business! I am trying...' She felt miserable, trying to appease him, yet stifle her own fury at being so insulted.

He cut her off with a gesture she had come to understand, a flat slicing movement of his hand in the air, as though to end something. 'Basta. Good night, Veronica. You will do well, I am sure. Only do not encourage that Mr Kelly.' He bent, and brushed his lips warmly over her cheek. 'I will see you next Thursday when I return.'

'Yes. Goodnight, Pietro,' she said. She was realizing she would be alone once more, in this gloomy unhappy mansion, with the miserable fretful widow nagging at her. 'Don't stay long, please. Please come back sooner if you can.' She put her hand on his arm anxiously. 'I don't know how I shall manage without you.' She was trying to tell him about her fears, but he misunderstood.

'I hope you are not the kind of woman who needs continual entertainment,' he said stiffly, a spark of anger in his eyes. 'You will not find it so in Florence. Think carefully before you decide on marrying an Italian!'

'I did not mean that! I did not!' She protested, and pressed his arm with her hand pleadingly. 'Please, Pietro, don't be angry with me.' Her voice broke on the words.

He bent again and this time brushed his lips against her mouth. Something like an instant flash of lightning seemed to tingle through her at his touch. Heat, warmth, light—all at once, shocking her.

'Of course, cara. We shall talk again. The trouble is we have not talked with each other enough. We must come to know each other.'

He left, and she returned to the drawing room, to sit in front of the fire, a victim of many emotions. Fear of something, a dark menacing fear of some unknown evil. Anger at Pietro for his insinuations about her and Andy.

And a soft hopeful dreamy feeling about her future life with Pietro, if they should come to love each other. She sat in front of the blazing, crackling warmth for a long time.

CHAPTER 2

Veronica awakened with a jerk of fright. Still mostly asleep, she stared wide-eyed into the dark greyness of her huge bedroom.

Something was there.

Someone was moving in the room.

She held her breath, tensely, listening. There was a shadow across the mirror, a black shadow —bending? Moving?

'Who's there?' she demanded, sitting up. She forced the words, her throat tight. 'Who's there? Who...'

A rush, a rustle. The door banged shut. Veronica shook with chill and reaction. Someone had been there. Why? Who?

She forced her cold body to move. She slid from the bed, put her small chilled feet into slippers, reached for her robe. By the time she had found her night candle and matches, she was shaking, so the first match blew out immediately.

She struck another, lit the candle. She picked up the holder, held it up to examine the room fearfully. The thin vague trembling light revealed no one.

She padded over to the huge mirrored dressing table, stumbled over the bench which was pushed aside from its usual position. She rubbed her knee automatically, stared incredulously at the dresser. Powder had spilled from its box, the small drawers were left as though they had been hastily opened and searched.

What was the person looking for? Jewellery? She kept little in the house. Most was in the huge safe at the Murray Jewellery shop in town.

She shuddered, closed the drawers, set the bench in place and returned to the warm nest of her bed.

Why? Why had someone come at night and searched her room? Anyone could easily have come in the daytime. Veronica's doors were never locked.

'They wanted to frighten me,' Veronica whispered to herself. She cuddled down in bed, drew the blankets around her shoulders. 'They want to scare me. Why? Who is doing this to me? Waking me at night, prowling around my room. Does it have anything to do

26

with father's death?'

She tried to settle down to sleep. But the black fears had come back with the ominous unknown presence in her bedroom. This was not the first time it had happened. Someone had come twice while her father lay dying.

And the mysterious death of her father had mingled with her fears until they were one, connected. Who had hated her father? Pietro had been in New York for more than six months, while her father's health gave way and he collapsed.

The speculations kept on stinging in her mind, prickles of memories, thorns of doubt. Pietro and the doctor had talked together several times, had stopped abruptly when she entered the room. Pietro was frankly enthusiastic about running the jewellery business, and had bluntly expressed his disbelief in Veronica's ability to run it alone. He didn't seem to think too highly of women in business.

She remembered he had said, 'No woman could run such a complex business. We can run it together. I have some ideas. I am going to change some practices. I... I...'

His words had switched from *we* to *I* with great ease.

'I won't doubt him! I won't!' She vowed it aloud, stubbornly, to the greyness of her room.

She willed herself to sleep, to find her nightmares full of vague fears, vague terrifying forms in the darkness.

In the morning, Jennie exclaimed over the chaos on the dresser, the spilled powder, the jewellery spilled with it, the disarranged brushes and combs.

'Jennie, tell nobody about this, nobody at all! Someone was in my room, but I won't be frightened.'

'Miss Veronica, you be careful!' Jennie whispered, her blue eyes rolling in alarm. 'Somebody means you harm!'

'Someone wants to scare me,' said Veronica firmly, stifling her own choking fears. 'That is all. In a few weeks I'll be married and on my way to Italy. Jennie, I want you to sleep in my room every night until I leave.'

'Sure I will, Miss. I can sleep on the day couch here,' said Jennie. 'Don't you fret. I sleep light, and nobody's going to come in and hurt you!'

Jennie was a pillar of strength to the troubled girl in the next weeks. She helped pack her possessions for the long trip to Italy, the sea voyage, the new life in a strange country. She packed clothes, gave advice, suggested purchases for that heathen place, as though Veronica were going to darkest Africa.

'And don't you worry about marriage, my dear. Your husband will teach you, and you don't need to worry. But I'll tell you something about men if you want.'

So Jennie told her tactfully, carefully, about men and other matters which the convent sisters had neglected to mention to their charges. Veronica was grateful to her practical maid, and the older woman treated her almost like a daughter as she prepared her for marriage. She would have hated to ask the distracted Sybil, and some of the things Jennie told her were very strange indeed—strange and exciting, and secretly thrilling.

While Pietro was out of the city, Veronica noticed that Giorgio and his father appeared every day. They wished to read some of the fine books in her father's library, they said. However, Giorgio looked at pictures in the books, and his father read a newspaper printed in Italian.

So Veronica suspected that her future husband had sent his relatives to watch over her. Protection? Did he suspect something? Or did he thing she was carrying on behind his back? In all events, she was grateful for their presence. They took lunch with her and gloomy Sybil, and made that meal easier. Giorgio volunteered to drive with her to the shop each afternoon, and waited with unusual patience for her to be finished and return with her.

Pietro called on her on Friday after his trip. He reported carefully, conscientiously on what he had discovered about the jewellery business there, and his plans for their business.

'More delicate jewellery,' she said thoughtfully, when he was finished. 'Yes, I thought so. My father and I had contemplated changes in our designs. What about the gem stones themselves? Is there a change in popularity?'

'Yes, they reported that jet is no longer in as much demand. Pearls are always popular, and they thought that would continue. The demand for garnets has risen. Diamonds are used with more restraint.'

They discussed orders for the shop in New York during their absence.

'I could return in midwinter and see how things are going,' said Pietro.

'No, I don't believe that will be necessary. Mr Jones worked with father for years. I think if we give him general directions, he will follow them faithfully.'

'It would be better if Andrew Kelly remained here,' said Pietro, choosing his words with care, his accent strong.

'I think he should learn more about the

30

Italian branch,' said Veronica, looking at the fire. She didn't want to say her true thoughts, that she wanted a friend around near her, in that strange unknown country of Italy, until she could adjust to her husband and his relatives and friends.

When she looked at Pietro's face again, it was stiff, his jaw jutting out. She sighed to herself. This was going to be difficult.

'Pietro, did you ask your cousin and uncle to come here? I am grateful because, though I have not told you, there is something I fear...'

He frowned, staring at her, his eyes lighting somewhat. 'Fear? What is it?'

She wasn't ready to voice anything yet. 'I don't know exactly. I have asked Jennie to sleep in my room. There is something... Oh, Pietro, don't let Sybil talk you into not marrying me!' she ended impulsively.

He said, more naturally, in some anger, 'She is trying to make trouble between us, I know it! She has told me you are reluctant to marry me. She had hinted you don't wish to go to Italy. Yes, I asked Giorgio and Uncle to come here, but to protect you. I too have some fears. Your father's death seemed strange to me.'

Impulsively she put her small hand on his big one as he leaned closer to her from his chair. 'Yes, it was strange. Oh, Pietro, I am counting

31

the days until we can get married! I want to leave this house! I am afraid here. And I do want to marry you. Father wished it. I wish it. Oh, please, don't listen to Sybil!'

His hands closed warmly about hers, he pressed them, spoke strongly. 'No, I won't listen to her. We must trust each other. Veronica, I do wish to marry you—very much.'

She hugged the words to her the next days, which were trying. Sybil was annoying, teasing her sometimes about the future. She said that in Italy Veronica couldn't have her own way, that women were kept under control as they should be. She hinted that Pietro would take over her life, her business, her money, as soon as they were married.

Once she said, 'Veronica, stay with me! You are so like your father, it comforts me. I miss him so much.'

If she had kept on in that vein, Veronica might have agreed to stay. She knew her step-mother was lonely, upset, fretting over the parting to come.

Dr Heinrich, who had attended her father, came to see her upon her request. He was not their regular family doctor. Sybil had quarrelled with kindly Dr Miller, and had produced her own doctor, to attend her husband the final six months of his life.

32

Sybil came down the stairs when the doctor arrived, and Veronica was relieved to see her. She did not want to be alone with the strange man she instinctively distrusted. 'Dr Heinrich, how good of you to come. Is Veronica ill?'

The German doctor stared keenly at Veronica, looked her up and down as she stood there in her pink muslin. 'No, she looks in the pink of health, like a girl about to marry, eh?' He said the words, staring at her in an unpleasant knowing way.

She flushed, asked him to come into the drawing room. Sybil followed them into the room, seated herself on the couch. Veronica smiled with relief, and patted Sybil's ready hand.

'Doctor, I asked you to come to tell me why my father died,' she said quietly. 'You have never told me!'

'Eh? Well, that is not necessary. You are a child,' he said, brusquely, and exchanged a quick look with Sybil.

'A child no longer. I am twenty, about to be married, and I am the head of a large jewellery business,' she said bravely. 'I wish to be told the truth, please. Why did my father die?'

He said, 'I don't know. He faded away. Why pursue the matter? There was something inside him, eating him away. You saw him die,' he added brutally, his dark eyes flashing. 'He was gravely ill, not wanting to live because of the pain. Surely, you didn't wish him to linger on, in his condition!'

Sybil gasped, 'Doctor, please!'

Veronica ignored the bait, and stuck to the main point. 'Gravely ill of what? What disease? Consumption? He did not have the symptoms.'

'There are many illnesses of which we doctors—I confess it—are ignorant,' said the German doctor ponderously. He tipped his fingers together, his black eyes gleaming at her. He still looked her up and down in a familiar way she disliked very much. 'I cannot tell you why he died. This is a mystery we shall probably never solve. In decades and centuries to come...'

She listened to him as though she believed him, let her stepmother argue with him. When he had left, she found her suspicions were stronger than ever.

As it happened, Andy Kelly appeared that afternoon to show her some new designs. He sensed her distress, and asked her what was wrong.

'Oh, Mr Kelly—may I call you Andy—I must tell someone, and I don't know what to do...'

'But of course!' He sat down in the big comfortable chair that had been her father's favourite. The door was closed. Sybil had left the house to go shopping.

Veronica told him in a low tone. 'I strongly suspect that my father was given something over several months or longer, something which eventually caused his death.'

'Poison?' snapped Andy, his blue eyes alert. 'Father thought...could it be that he was poisoned?'

'I suspect that,' said Veronica, with a sigh of despair. 'Andy, I suspect that he was poisoned, and that if I remain here in New York with my stepmother, we too are in grave danger!'

There. The words were out. The fears and suspicions that had eaten her as that strange illness had eaten her father.

Andy Kelly stared at her gravely. She remembered that his father was one of the three lawyers of her father.

'What did your father think about this?' she asked, in a whisper.

'He was puzzled, wondering. He said he never saw anyone fade away like that.'

'Yes, yes, that is what I mean! Oh, Andy, how can I discover the truth? Is it so dreadful to distrust the doctor? Would he do such a thing?'

'I don't know, but there is a way to find out

35

if your father was poisoned. I can—if you permit it.'

'How can I? Tell me!' She drew closer on the couch, and they put their heads together like conspirators and whispered.

'I have a friend in medical school. He is advanced, and he has told me things. We can —Veronica, this is most unpleasant. We can dig up his body, your father's body, and—cut it open, and he will examine it, and discover the cause of death!'

Veronica put her hand over her mouth convulsively. She felt violently ill. Andy stared at her anxiously.

'I'm sorry. I shouldn't have told you—of course you won't want this,' he said.

She got control of herself firmly. 'Yes—yes,' she choked. 'If he is willing to do it—and you will let me know. Go ahead, Andy. Find out. I must know...'

'I can't be sure of this. I think he can discover it. It's the only way we can try—'

'Who is there in the dark with you, Veronica?' The deep voice sent them flying apart like guilty children. Pietro came into the open, stared at them sternly. His face was a study in jealousy and fury.

Andy stood up with some semblance of dignity. 'I must go now, Veronica. I'll do

36

as you suggested...'

He started to leave the room. Pietro silently lifted the sheaf of untouched designs from the table and handed them to the tall blond man. Andy flushed red, grabbed the papers and escaped.

Pietro closed the door after him. Veronica stood guiltily in her place, gazing at her angry fiancé.

'Why was he here?' Pietro, with cold restraint, asked her. 'I have told you I don't wish you to visit with him. He is in love with you.'

'In love! No. He brought the designs, we discussed the designs,' said Veronica. She was a very bad liar. 'He doesn't love me, he doesn't! The designs,' she repeated, like an idiot. 'The new designs...'

He stared at her in silence as though reading her mind. She waited for his fury to break over her, a furious tempest.

'I believe,' he said, too softly, too gently, 'that it is going to be unexpectedly difficult for us to trust each other!'

He turned and walked out, and left the house. She did not see him for four days, during which she shook with fear, and cried in her pillow at night. Her nightmares were horrible, full of darkness and greyness and strange shapes and chill menace.

Jennie tried to soothe her, thinking she was fearful of the coming marriage, but Veronica would not be soothed. She had put herself in a very compromising position with Andy, and Pietro might never trust her again. What kind of a marriage would this be? A jealous husband, a friend whom she couldn't explain, and a fear that haunted her. Did Andy love her? He had seemed like a friend, a good sturdy friend.

The wedding took place on a bright sunny morning in late September. The Saturday wedding of wealthy American girl to an Italian duke attracted a curious crowd of bystanders. Few guests had been invited, in keeping with the mourning period for her father.

As Veronica walked down the long aisle of the Catholic church, in her billowing white dress, the long train, peeping through the lacy veil of her wedding attire, she was shaking with weariness and desperation. She was tired after sleepless nights, worried about her future marriage to a stranger, even more worried about Sybil.

Sybil had gone out several times, discreetly, with Dr Heinrich. Was the doctor planning to complete his conquest of the widow? Was this why he had plotted, planned, done something to Frank Murray—in order to marry the wealthy bereaved woman? Would a doctor, a man in the respected medical profession, do such a thing? Had Sybil ever encouraged him to think she would marry him?

Or was poor Sybil as much of a victim as her late husband? Would the doctor marry her —then get rid of her? Veronica shuddered. Maybe she was doing the wrong thing to desert Sybil. Sybil might need her desperately.

As Veronica walked along, Andy's father holding her arm lightly, her flower girl in front of her, she searched for Pietro's form at the head of the aisle. There he was, waiting at the altar, correctly attired in morning attire, a white carnation in his buttonhole. She smelled the white roses of her bouquet, felt the red plush carpet under her white slippers, watched for the first sight of Pietro's face. He was her only hope, her only escape, the only security she had left in the world. For if her father had been in Dr Heinrich's way—so was Veronica.

As she came, Pietro turned, and looked at her, and the look twisted her heart. It was so cold, so distant, not even a smile on his lips.

The priest met them at the altar, the ceremony began. The mass was long, and Veronica's knees grew weary on the cushions as they took communion together, promised their promises.

'Will I be happy? Can I make him happy? Oh, Lord, help me,' she prayed. She scarcely heard the words of the ceremony, the prayers, the blessing. Frantically her mind searched for some sign of hope, some sign of blessing from God on this strange marriage.

She must not be superstitious, she thought, she must not look for omens, it was wrong. Yet she found herself watching, waiting, for something, some sign that all would be well.

She heard Pietro's voice, his accent strong. Oh, he is angry, she thought. He is still angry with me!

She couldn't blame him, but she couldn't explain either. She couldn't tell him what she had commissioned her friend to do, how Andy and his medical friend would take out her father's body from the earth, and cut it—

Suddenly she felt sick, and swayed on the cushion. Pietro's hand shot out, and he held her elbow carefully as she recovered her balance. His hand was warm and reassuring, his face anxious as he looked at her.

She nodded slightly, smiled a little. His face relaxed.

That was the only good moment of the day. Later, at the hotel, in the long reception, she felt weary again, weary and heartsick.

Sybil stood beside her in the reception line,

still wearing her black mourning silk. It seemed an ill omen in that gay occasion, thought Veronica. She wished Sybil had worn grey, or even green, or blue, for her stepdaughter's wedding.

Andy Kelly approached the line, looked guiltily at Pietro, shook hands hastily, and went on to speak to Veronica.

His words were conventional. 'May you be very happy—my best wishes—' His blue eyes betrayed his real thoughts, hurt and defiant.

She clasped his hand tightly with hers. Was Pietro right? Did Andy love her? She wished things had been different. Then she saw Pietro watching them, and dropped Andy's hand too hastily. 'Thank you, Andy,' she said.

Sybil was looking at them, looking at their nearness, as though wakening slowly to some idea. Her black silk skirts rustled as she moved closer as though to overhear. Behind her, too close, stood Dr Heinrich, a dark shadow of a man.

'I'll see you in Italy, then, Veronica,' said Andy.

'Yes, in Florence,' said Veronica.

He moved on, and she thought that her last friend was gone.

At the end of the brief wedding ceremony before the mass, when Pietro had kissed her, he had been so abrupt, so cold. His mouth had scarcely brushed hers, she thought.

Sybil said, gaily, to Pietro, 'I can't imagine what you think of all this ceremony, the cake and eating and drinking. It must seem so different to you.'

'It is much the same. The mass, the feasting,' he said, as though indifferent to everything.

'But Italy is so different, there you can manage things as you wish, Pietro, can't you?' said Sybil, smiling a light mocking smile. She had flung herself out of her dark morbid mood into a maddening teasing one that Veronica disliked even more. 'Our American girls are sometimes headstrong. They have to learn to obey their husbands!'

Veronica stiffened. She waited for Pietro to deny this, to say he loved her (even though he didn't), to say something nice about her.

Pietro shrugged. 'Things are different in Italy,' he said, and that was all.

The ceremonies went on and on, the guests flowed in and out again. Veronica stood and stood, miserably aware of her angry jealous husband, her moody unhappy stepmother, her own loneliness. She had hoped that she and Pietro would come to love each other.

That chance seemed remote.

CHAPTER 3

It was raining as the ship was tugged slowly out of its berth in the New York harbour, and began steaming out to the Atlantic Ocean. Rain spattered on the windows of the grand suite of Veronica and her new husband. Not a trace of sunlight, nothing but the grey sky overhead, the grey seas beyond.

She sat on the edge of the bed, and could have cried. Pietro was as cold and stormy as the weather! She was leaving everything she had known, everything familiar and warm and comfortable, to go off into the unknown.

Even Jennie was left behind. The good maid who had known her since she was a baby had wept bitterly as Veronica had helped her fasten the suitcases and trunks shut.

'Who will look after you? Who'll take care of my baby? All alone in that heathen country!'

Pietro had said there were plenty of maids there, no need to have Jennie. She could stay on in the Murray household, be there on Veronica's trips home. If Sybil didn't fire her, his new wife had thought bitterly.

But he was her husband, and the master of her life now. Sitting on the edge of the bed, staring at her suitcases, she sighed deeply.

Finally she stood up, unfastened her hat and laid it aside. She took off her full dark cloak, and laid in on a chair. Pietro had the adjoining cabin. They shared a bathroom. The two days after their marriage had been spent in separate rooms of her old home packing, rushing from place to place, making final plans for the long absence.

She had scarcely seen Pietro. Not at all at night! He hadn't acted much like a husband. She had told Jennie to keep on sleeping in her bedroom for those nights.

But now they would be alone. The dreaded moments were approaching. She felt fear, a strange tingling fear.

She unpacked one of the suitcases, laid the underclothes in drawers. She staggered as the ship lurched under her feet, and the empty suitcases slid across and banged against the door. This was her first trip on a large ocean liner. It felt strange, to hear the throb of the motors, feel the sliding motion under her, to brace herself against the slight sway as the ship leaned first to one side and then the other.

Pietro knocked briefly on the door between their cabins.

'Come in!'

She looked at him as he entered. Still the same cold reserved expression. Would he always look like that at her?

'One does not dress formally the first night at sea,' he said, in the slightly bossy manner she disliked. 'The dress you are wearing will do quite well. I have signed us up for the late sitting this evening.'

'Very well,' she forced herself to say quietly. During this past year she had made so many decisions herself, it was a little frustrating and irritating to be told what to do. It reminded her too much of the convent and the nuns. So many rules, so many regulations, so much anger at the infringement of the least one—'I have unpacked enough for the next few days. When do you wish to go?'

'We will go to the lounge now, and meet Uncle Teodosio and Giorgio. We will go to dinner together later.'

She bit her lips, looked about the cabin seeking an excuse to linger. They would talk, perhaps in Italian, leaving her out. Was she going to be put in a corner alone, for the rest of her days?

'You will need a shawl,' said Pietro, more kindly. 'It is chilly in the hallways. Where is your white one?'

45

'Oh—in another suitcase,' she said, rather happily. She bent down to unfasten it.

'Allow me,' he said, and unlocked it and opened it for her. The white shawl was on the top layer, and he drew it out, and closed the case again.

He set the shawl about her shoulders, managing not to touch her once with his fingers. She hugged it about herself. She felt chilly again. The rose and white muslin dress rustled as she followed him down the hallways, through a bewildering maze of doors and halls and lounges, until he came to the one he wanted. She wondered if she could ever find her way alone.

As they approached Pietro's relatives, the ship lurched. Pietro caught her arm quickly. She staggered, regained her balance.

The men stood up politely. Giorgio held a chair for her.

'It is going to be a bad storm,' said Pietro's cousin, as though happy about it.

'Yes, mid-September,' said Pietro. 'I expected it. Well, when we get to the Mediterranean, it will be all right again. That is usually protected.'

Veronica sat and listened to them discuss the coming storm. The ship kept lurching and sliding under her feet, her chair tipped from side to side, making her gasp. When they rose to go to the dining room, she could scarcely stand. Pietro held her on one side, Teodosio on the other.

To sit and eat became agony. Course followed course. The men ate hungrily, talked sometimes in Italian. Politely, they addressed a few words to her in English. She looked about to see if any familiar face was aboard. Few people were there in the first class dining room.

She knew no one. Some of the women were pale. One held her throat, then got up and made a dash for the door.

'Seasick,' said Giorgio, without much interest.

'Oh,' said Veronica. She felt nausea rising to her own throat. All this food—she wanted a cup of tea and her own soft bed at home! She wanted to stand on a floor that didn't slide from under her feet. She wanted to be—to be alone!

She couldn't eat any more. Pietro urged her to eat more; she shook her head.

'The courses—so many,' she said, faintly, in excuse. She was fighting nausea, a real nausea rising in her throat. What would Pietro say if she too had to dash for the door? Where would she go? Where was the nearest ladies' room? Should she go outside and vomit over the rail? The more she tried not to think about it, the

47

more she thought about it.

The men wanted brandy in the lounge after dinner. 'If you will excuse me—' she said. 'I believe I'll go to my cabin. I am quite weary—'

The men smiled, significantly, and Giorgio looked at Pietro.

'Of course. We will retire,' said Pietro, and took her arm possessively.

'I can find my way,' she said, not really sure about that.

He acted as though he hadn't heard her. In front of the men's grins, he led her out the door of the dining room, through lounges, hallways, doors, briefly outside, then inside again, on still another route back to their cabins. She would never learn this ship, she thought, in despair.

Walking made her feel better, though. She didn't feel as sick as she had while sitting in that chair in the dining room, smelling the food, rocking slowly, involuntarily, side to side.

Pietro took her into her cabin. 'Take your time, cara,' he said. 'I am patient. We have all the time in the world, now, with no outsiders to bother us.'

He smiled down at her kindly, and went to his cabin. She froze. He meant—he meant—to come to her tonight!

'Oh, I can't do it, not tonight,' she whispered involuntarily to herself. 'I feel so awful—oh, what shall I do?'

She undressed. There was nothing else to do. She was married. She had to submit to her husband's wishes. This was 1893. Women were not so confined and restricted as in previous centuries, she thought, but there were still some fields where a husband reigned supreme.

She washed, bracing herself against the wash stand in the small bathroom. She put on the fine cambric nightdress with the clusters of fine tucks front and back, with the three inch lace ruffle around her throat. The pink colour became her.

Then she went to her cabin, and got into bed, and pulled up the covers tightly. The bed wasn't very wide. Would it be wide enough? Pietro was rather tall. What had Jennie said about it? Submit, she had said. Let him lead you. Oh, God, thought Veronica, oh, dear Lord, I'm afraid I'm going to be sick. Very very sick.

The bed was swaying, even though it was nailed to the floor. The floor was swaying. She was swaying, dizzy. Waves of nausea swept through her. Her stomach churned.

Pietro was washing. She could hear the sounds of the water, heard him humming. He wasn't sick at all. Somehow that made her feel resentful.

She pressed her hand over her stomach to quiet it. The stomach muscles quivered.

The longer she lay there, the sicker she felt.

The humming stopped. A door opened, closed. She shut her eyes tight. She felt rather than saw Pietro come over her bed. He bent down. She felt his fingers touch her cheek.

'Cara,' he said softly. He drew back the covers, and started to get into bed.

She said something, wildly, 'Oh—don't—I'm sick!' She lurched up in the bed. She pushed him aside, furiously, out of her way, and made a dash for the bathroom. She slammed the door, and was sick, violently.

She cried as she was sick. She was so horribly embarrassed, so upset, so awfully nauseated. She couldn't bear to think what he would say...

He knocked on the bathroom door. It was locked. 'Cara, let me in.'

'I'm sick,' she wailed.

'I know. Let me help you,' he said, patiently.

She could not endure to let him see her being sick. 'No! Let me alone!'

Silence. She sobbed, almost fell as the ship lurched. She hated the ship, it was alive, evil, monstrous, about to gobble her up, make her insane. If it didn't stop bouncing around like this...

It didn't stop. She was sick, she lost all her supper. Finally she was too weak to stand. She unlocked the door, went into her cabin. Pietro was sitting on a chair, waiting, his face pale and set.

She staggered over to the bed. Right now, she didn't care if he saw her or not. She crawled in, pulled up the blankets.

'Do you feel better?' he asked, coldly, she thought.

She sniffled. 'Some. Oh, Pietro, I want to go home!' she wailed.

'We are going home. To Italy,' he said. He got up, came over to the bed. She stiffened, Surely, he would not... He pulled the blankets up more securely around her. 'I will prop open my door. If you need me in the night, call me.'

He took one of the suitcases and propped open the door between their cabins. She peeped at him, as he moved about his cabin. He looked angry and upset. Right now, she didn't care. Sometime later, when this sickness was over, she probably would care very much, she thought.

She was sick in the night, but she didn't call him. She endured it, went back to bed, huddled miserably, hating the voyage, hating the marriage, hating everyone.

Sometime that night, she slept a little. She

wakened to find the sunshine streaming in the windows leading to the small private deck outside their suite. Pietro was out there, sitting in a chair, looking out at the sea.

She felt a little better, more cheerful. Then she sat up. 'Ooohhh,' she groaned. She lay down again. Her stomach heaved.

Pietro came in presently. 'Do you feel better?' he asked.

She moved her head back and forth on the pillow. Her blonde hair streamed wildly about her face. It was usually neatly braided, but she had not stopped to arrange it last night. Now she didn't care what she looked like.

'I'll bring you some breakfast,' he said.

'No—no food,' she groaned.

'You must eat something. It will make you feel better,' he said patiently. 'Later you will come up on deck. Fresh air helps very much.'

She closed her eyes. He was a stupid unfeeling brute, a man. He didn't understand her.

He left. Later he came back with an orange and tea and a soft white roll. She looked at it, and felt sick again.

'Try some tea,' he urged. 'Just a little tea.'

He helped her sit up. He spooned tea into her mouth as though she were a child. It did help a little. But when he urged her to dress and go on deck, she looked at him as though he were mad.

'Get up and dressed! I can't, Pietro! I can't move out of this room! Don't you realize...' she wailed. 'Oooohhh—why can't you be sick too? Then you'd know how miserable I am!'

For the first time, he grinned, widely. It changed his whole face, made him seem much younger and happier. 'I'm sorry, cara, if it would make you well, I would be happy to get sick. But I do not usually become seasick, I am so sorry.'

She sighed. She wished she could laugh with him. He sat on the edge of the bed, and patted her hand comfortingly.

'Don't worry, Veronica. It will soon be over, then you will feel fine again. Believe me, if you would come up on deck, you would be much better. The fresh air helps one immensely.'

'I can't,' she said. 'Please don't ask me, Pietro. I just want to lie here and...and rest.' She had almost said, 'and die,' she felt so miserable.

He left, to go out on deck, at her urging. She lay, half-asleep. She felt better to lie still. But whenever she had to get up, to go to the bathroom, she felt violently seasick again.

He returned, to urge her to dress and go on deck. She refused. He was a little angry at her stubbornness. She looked at him, and hardened her heart. He could not boss her in this! She knew when she was sick.

'Just please let me alone, please let me alone,' she asked angrily, and turned her back on him, flopping on the bed.

'All right,' he said, and walked out.

He left her alone for hours. Unreasonably, she was furious with him, for granting her wish. He didn't care if she was lonely, away from all her friends. She wept, with self pity.

That night, he propped the door open again. But she didn't need to get up. She felt somewhat better. Again the next day, he urged her up on deck. She refused. She felt safe and warm in bed, alone. She wasn't sure what would happen if she ventured out on deck.

'You cannot stay here all the time,' he said reasonably. 'You must get up sometime. Now that you are better...'

'I'm not well yet!'

He sighed, and left her again. She felt restless, more alert, feeling better, yet afraid to venture out.

That evening, after he had gone to dinner, she finally got up. She didn't feel too bad, just a little dizzy. She took a bath, while he was gone, and felt much better, more alive and happy. Maybe this wouldn't be so bad after all.

She went out to the sheltered deck, the tiny

area outside their suite, and smelled the fresh sea air. The ocean still churned at her feet, the deck still swayed. But she felt more sure of her footing now.

She sat alone for a long time, as the dusk covered the ocean, and the lights on the ship began to blaze cheerily. Where was everyone? Why didn't Pietro return to her? She had dressed, as he had requested. Now he didn't come back.

It was chilly on deck. She went back inside, but the room felt tight and confining now. She found her black thick cloak and put it on, covering her head. She had managed to braid her hair, but the braids hung down her back. She looked like a schoolgirl, not like a married woman. She didn't want people to see her like this, but she didn't have the energy to tie up her hair in a beautiful dignified coronet.

She walked out of the cabin, and reached for the nearest railing. A steward appeared as though by magic. He smiled at her. 'Better now, madame? You are better?'

'Yes, much better. I'm going out on deck,' she said, with much more assurance than she felt.

'Allow me to help you. You wish to go where your husband is? He is on the sports deck, madame.'

She wondered how he knew that. Servants always seemed to know everything. She accepted his aid, and made it up the steep ladders to an upper deck. Lights glowed at the front of the ship, at the back also. Dimmer lights gleamed from the windows of the lounges along the sides of the decks.

He walked slowly with her, holding her arm politely, carefully, advising her where to put her feet on the steps, how to hold on.

'I will obtain a deck chair for you, if you wish,' he said, as she paused on the long walk.

'Thank you, that would be nice,' she said, and leaned against the rail to wait.

'Shall I find your husband for you, and advise him to come?' the steward said, returning to her in a few minutes.

She heard a burst of laughter from another deck. 'No—no, I'll just sit here for a while,' she said quickly. She felt a pang of jealousy. Was Pietro playing and having fun while she was sick? 'They are—over there?'

'On the sports deck, at that end, there, madame, just one flight down, at the back of the ship.' He pointed. She let him help her to the deck chair, covered her with a blanket and departed, satisfied that he had achieved his purpose in getting her up on deck.

She sat there in the dimness, watching the

waves of the mighty Atlantic Ocean rolling and rolling endlessly. She felt very small as she sat, feeling the rolling of the large ship, a small chip on the ocean, tossing and responding to the least wave of the ocean.

How little it was, how very small she was, she thought. A pawn of fate, a small thing tossed about by forces unknown, by forces stronger than she was.

She half lay in the deck chair, resting after the long walk. She felt almost hungry, and thought of the orange in her cabin. She would have welcomed the sweet juice of that orange...

Where was Pietro? How long was he going to play? Or would he go back to their suite and find her gone? What would he say? He wouldn't get jealous, think she was meeting someone... No, there was no one to meet. She had left all her friends behind her; she knew no one on board this ship.

Loneliness rolled over her. She huddled up in the blanket. But this was ridiculous, she told herself. All she had to do was find Pietro. He was right there, nearby.

Finally she got up. It was dark now, and the deck was wet and slippery with ocean spray. She went over to the railing, and hung on to it as she walked back toward the lighted lower deck.

Only a few people had walked past her as she had sat on the deck chair. A few women wrapped in dark cloaks, their voices silvery in the night air. A few men, their voices rumbling, cigar smoke rolling from them. Talking, laughing, in another world.

Her foot slipped on the deck. She paused to regain her balance, caught her breath. She looked down, down into the ocean as it rolled and pounded against the ship. How dark, how black and menacing it looked, with only a few white curls of spume on its waves. It must be very cold down there, very cold and deep. How deep it must be.

She went further, slowly, watching her steps. She clung to the rail, the wind was keener now as she moved from the protection of the side deck. Her cloak blew back, her head was exposed. She clutched at the hood pulling at it.

She reached the end of the deck, clung to the railing as she peered down. Some men and women were gathered on the lower deck just under her gaze. There was Giorgio, Teodosio; there was Pietro, laughing down at a pert dark-haired woman! Pietro, laughing with a woman, now taking a long stick and pushing at something that slammed along the deck. There was a burst of applause. Pietro beamed, he seemed happier than she had ever seen him.

She watched them for a time. She thought he might look up, she would wave and smile, he would come up the steps beside her, and hold her arm, and talk to her.

Pietro did not look up. Giorgio disappeared inside. Teodosio was standing there near Pietro, wearing a black cap and a relaxed look such as she had not seen before. How happy they all were, to be returning home to Italy, to be playing, to be away from her, that cold American heiress Pietro had married.

Her hood flew back again at another gust of the wind. She left it this time, letting the wind play through her hair. It felt good, cold and pure and salty, full of the sea.

She dreamed as she stood there, leaning against the rail, watching her husband play. Someday, she would be friends with him, he would understand her, he would be gentle with her...

So suddenly that she was stunned, a push came.

A push on her shoulders and back. A hard push. A firm strong push.

Hands on her, pushing.

She screamed, her throat tearing with the agony of the scream.

She lurched, grabbed wildly at the railing. She had noticed that this rail was one that had a caution sign on it. It was where they loaded, and the rail would open—

It opened, and she lurched again. The ship swayed, she was going—going—over—into the sea.

She forced herself backwards. She caught a glimpse of something black—a figure—behind her.

She fell backwards. Down the stairs. Screaming—screaming, she fell on the stairs, the iron steps biting into her back, painful against her shoulders, her hips, her arms. her head. Her head, banging...

Arms caught her, strong arms plucked her from the stairs. Arms caught her, and held her tight. They both fell to the deck, but the strong figure was beneath her, protecting.

She lay, stunned, unable to speak.

The figure crawled out, cradled her, held her tightly. 'Veronica...' said a strange deep voice. Breathless voice. 'Cara...cara...'

It was Pietro. He had caught her. She tried to speak, to thank him. Her voice was gone.

'Her eyes are open,' said a woman's shrill voice. 'My God, if you hadn't caught her...'

'Hold her up. I have some smelling salts,' said another woman's voice.

Strong fumes invaded her nostrils. She squirmed, turned her head, felt senses returning. She pressed her face against Pietro's coat, shuddering.

'What happened? What happened?' It was Giorgio's voice.

'She fell down the steps,' said Pietro. 'I heard her scream. Madre di Dios, those steps. Is her head bleeding?'

Careful hands poked around her head. She moaned as they found a soft painful place.

'Bruised,' said Giorgio's familiar voice. 'Try her arms...try her legs. See if she broke anything.'

They straightened out her arms and legs. She felt chilled as they held open the cloak. Finally someone was satisfied.

'No, bruises only. Cara, do you hear me? Cara?' It was Pietro, gently folding the cloak about her, holding her closely to his warm body.

She tried to speak, tried again. Succeeded. 'Pietro,' she whispered.

'Yes, cara.' His face bent close to hers. 'What happened? I should have made you wait. I should have come up with you. Why did you come up on deck alone? You must have been dizzy?'

She looked into his dark eyes, his anxious eyes. She tried to say she had been pushed. The words wouldn't come. Just beyond his face was

Giorgio's, a small mocking smile on his lips. His suit was black, his tall figure in black...

The figure had been black, dressed in black. The person who had pushed her.

Words wouldn't come. She couldn't speak.

'If she had fallen a few feet further forward,' said a man's voice, with heavy authority, a British accent, 'she would have gone right into the sea. In this storm...'

'Hush,' said a woman. 'Don't frighten her.'

She would have gone into the sea, she thought. She shivered, violently, with more than a chill. She would have fallen into the black ocean, the devouring evil menacing ocean, those dark waves, those deep terrible waves. She would have been swallowed up into the ocean. And in this storm no one would have been able to rescue her!

She would have died. As someone wanted her to die.

Someone had pushed her. Someone in black had meant for her to die in that ocean, to drown in the dark cold waters of the sea.

'Oh, Pietro,' she muttered, and began to cry.

'Take her below,' said Teodosio, authoritatively. 'She must rest. She has been severely shocked.'

'Yes, yes, take her below. Take her to her cabin.'

The men lifted her up, and carried her downstairs. The doctor came, and gave her something that made her sleep. But even in the dreams, she cried out, and Pietro came and held her gently, because she thought she was being pushed into the dark waters of the ocean.

CHAPTER 4

She was covered with bruises, but no worse, the doctor told Veronica the next day. She stared at him, but said nothing. When he had left, Pietro helped her to go out to their own small portion of the deck, just outside their suite.

He settled her carefully into a deck chair, then sat down in the next one. His face was drawn, anxious.

'Cara, do you feel like talking a little?' he asked, very gently.

She nodded. 'If you wish,' she said, wearily. Whenever she closed her eyes she saw that menacing figure in black. Her sleep had been broken, her mind was still confused, as though it too was covered with bruises.

'Were you dizzy last evening when you fell?'

'No,' she said flatly. She looked him full in the face. 'Pietro, I was pushed. Someone from behind me pushed me.'

He did not say she was crazy or feverish. He only nodded, his dark eyes clouded. 'I thought so too,' he said simply. 'I heard you scream. I looked up and saw your blonde head. Behind you was someone in black. And that person did not grab you, or catch you. He turned away and ran...'

She relaxed with a great sigh of relief. 'Oh, Pietro, you saw him too! I thought I was mad or having delusions. What did he look like? Why would anyone try to kill me?'

He shook his head, slowly, leaned over to tuck the blanket up to her chin, over her shoulders. His touch was caressing. 'I did not see his face. He wore something black, something which covered him completely. He was tall, looming behind you. Oh, cara, I went through hell as I saw you falling...'

'That was why you were so quick. You saw me start to fall?'

'Yes. I jumped for the stairs, was up several steps when you had reached me. I was able to break the fall, thank God!'

She smiled at him shyly. 'Thank you, Pietro. I am so grateful. And for believing me. I was almost afraid to say anything, to tell anyone.

They would think me crazy...'

'You must not be afraid to tell me anything,' he said, rather severely. 'I am your husband, your protector. It is my duty to know everything about you. Why would anyone attempt to kill you?'

In spite of his bossy tone, she was pleased at his concern. 'That is what I do not know, Pietro. You see, I suspect that perhaps my father also was killed, that maybe his death was not an accident.'

He frowned, waited for her to say more. But she didn't want to say much until she heard from Andy. She might be wrong, unjust to the strange Dr Heinrich whom she distrusted. She had no evidence to point to him.

'So then are there vendettas in the United States also?' he asked.

'Vendettas! What do you mean?'

'I mean, when a member of the family injures the member of another family, revenge is taken, and then revenge for that, and so on, until the matter is ended, or everyone in one family is dead,' he explained. She shuddered.

'But that would be dreadful!' she said.

'You are pale, cara. We will speak no more about it now.' He said it with decision, leaned back and closed his eyes. She had to rest also, because he wouldn't let her say anymore, just shushed her firmly and told her to be quiet.

She was faintly amused by his possessive manner. She cuddled down into the blankets and slept a while, wakened to find him still near her, watching the sea.

He stayed near her all that day. A steward brought their lunches to them, then tea, then dinner. Giorgio stopped by several times to enquire how Veronica was. He did not urge them to come upstairs to the deck or lounge. He too seemed concerned, and he and Pietro talked a while in low tones in Pietro's cabin.

That night, he calmly went to bed with her. She was rather shaken by that. He made no attempt to force his love on her, but just held her in his arms and told her to sleep.

'The bed isn't very big,' she said feebly.

'Shush. Go to sleep. I will take care of you,' he said.

It took her a while to drift off to sleep. She wasn't used to feeling a man so close to her in bed, to rest her head on a man's shoulder and upper arm, to be so intensely aware of a man's presence and his body.

She finally slept, still aware of his nearness even in her dreams. It was comforting, he was so solid and protective.

In the morning, he was gone, but she heard him singing in the bathroom, something in

Italian, something from an opera, she thought.

All that day, they stayed in their cabin, talking, or sitting on the deck that was their own. The doctor came again, examined her, said she would recover quickly, gave her an ointment for the more prominent bruises. He was more curious today about how the accident had happened.

'I fell down the stairs,' said Veronica flatly. Pietro volunteered nothing more than that.

'And you have been seasick,' said the doctor.

'That is right,' she said.

They were still in the Atlantic Ocean, and the ocean was still behaving in a violent manner, heaving the ship from side to side, up and down. But she was becoming accustomed to this, and it did not bother her the way it had at first.

'When we get to Lisbon, we will go ashore and ride about in a carriage. You will be interested in Lisbon,' said Pietro.

'Tell me about Lisbon,' she asked.

He told her about it, about how the city had been founded more than two thousand years before, how the sailors had stopped there on their ancient travels, about the forts, the docks, the houses, the exotic gardens.

He found a book, and read it to her, all about Lisbon and Portugal. Then he began to tell her about Florence, about their future home, the Villa d'Oro up on the hillside, and his sister Camilla. She was evidently much younger than he, a pet of the Cavalcanti men, perhaps spoiled, thought Veronica. Pietro told her how pretty she was, how she was not allowed to go out without a chaperon, how lonely she became, how happy she was that Veronica was coming.

Veronica wasn't so sure that she and Camilla would get along well. When a girl had been spoiled by the men in her life, she might not welcome a newcomer. It would be nice to have a girl friend in the Villa d'Oro but she resolved not to be disappointed if Camilla did not like her.

Pietro slept with her again that night, evidently determined not to leave her for a minute. This time he kissed her before they slept, touching her cheek and mouth with his lips.

'You are a very beautiful girl, cara,' he said, murmuring the words, with his accent strong. 'So lovely, pretty...'

He touched her gently with his hand, and she shivered a little at the way he moved his hand down over her. But again he did not try to force his love on her.

She was rather disappointed, rather relieved. The next day, Giorgio and Teodosio evidently talked Pietro into coming up on deck with her. She had heard them discussing the matter at length in his cabin, their passionate Italian voices rising and falling like a trio in opera. Pietro came to her with the decision.

'We shall go up to the lounge for a while, cara, if you feel strong enough. Later we might go on deck, but I shall remain with you. You need not fear. Giorgio and my uncle shall also remain near you.'

'I'm sure no one would dare come near me with all of you protecting me,' she said, a little amused.

'Cara, this is not humorous!' he said sternly. 'Whoever tried once will try again. You must be careful!'

She sobered at once, her mouth drooping. He was quite right. Someone had succeeded in murdering her father, she was beginning to believe that firmly. Someone might have the same intentions toward her.

'Thank you, Pietro,' she told him, more humbly. 'It is hard to believe that someone... wants to kill me. I will be careful.' She caught his hand, pressed it to her cheek impulsively. 'You make me feel safe, so I almost forget the danger.'

His eyes sparkled, he leaned closer to her, caressed her cheek with his hand. Then Giorgio came into the cabin without knocking. Veronica wanted to slap him!

'Oh, excuse me. You wished to go up on deck?' The suave sophisticated cousin looked rather embarrassed. 'I can return later.'

'No, we can go up now. I think I would like to eat in the dining room today,' said Veronica quickly. She managed to smile at him. Pietro was fond of him, she was determined to like him also.

'Good, good, that will make you feel better, people around you, yes, si, si,' said Giorgio, pleased. 'That is better, eh, Pietro?'

They went up to the lounge, Pietro at Veronica's side, Giorgio and his father following like two stern guardians. She did feel safer! And it was better to be with people, to hear the chatter, the voices in English, Spanish, Italian, German, French, all around her. It was interesting to listen in to conversations, to catch the words, to translate the languages she knew a little.

The men hovered around her, though Giorgio kept looking longingly at a blonde English girl who had evidently caught his attention. 'We will play tennis again tomorrow,' he said to his father, in answer to a question, in Italian.

Veronica was amused, but did not reveal she

understood them. The longer she waited to tell her husband she had learned some Italian, the more difficult it was to confess.

They walked on deck, for a short distance, trailed by their faithful relatives. She kept watching nervously for a figure, tall, in a black cloak, but it was impossible. Everyone wore cloaks against the cold Atlantic wind, some wore cloaks of black, some grey, some Scotch plaids. And many of the men were quite tall.

'Do you recognize...?' Pietro murmured once.

She shook her head.

They went in to dinner, and she was amazed at the splendour of the dining room and the many courses. She had been too dazed and ill that first night to enjoy anything. Tonight, she looked about, at the splendidly dressed diners in First Class, at the attentive waiters, the decorations, the formally correct officers.

She was wearing her blue silk dress, at Pietro's request. With it, she wore her best strand of pearls, a tiny tiara of pearls, a gold bracelet and her wedding rings.

'You are the loveliest woman here,' Pietro murmured in her ear as he held her chair for her.

She smiled. He was very flattering. She could see many women more elegant and stunnng

71

than she was. She was very small, only five foot two, though her figure had been praised sometimes, and her face was the perfect oval now mentioned in the fashion pages as the best shape. Her blonde hair was coiled about her head, the tiara perched at the front over a wave. When she had looked in the mirror, she had thought she looked her best, her face creamy and pink, her mouth a soft red. But she was not stunning, she knew that. She did not have the height and commanding look of a stunning woman.

Still...If Pietro was pleased, that was all she cared about.

In the lounge after dinner, several persons came up to speak. Pietro introduced them, the blonde English girl, her parents, an Italian business man who had known her father, a French couple who chatted gaily half in English, half in French, a heavy German count who frowned when he spoke.

Veronica sat back and let her men carry the conversation. Giorgio gazed fondly at the English girl, she fluttered her lashes demurely. Veronica wished she could share the moment with a girl friend, this conquest of suave Giorgio. Though it might be that he was easily conquered, and easily lost! He was older than Pietro, and unmarried.

Pietro was gallant, and uninterested in the women. He spoke more readily to the business men. Teodosio spoke little, he found it an effort to speak in English, Veronica thought. He chattered readily enough when he found an Italian friend.

Then a soft voice murmured in her ear as she sat beside Pietro. Veronica whirled around, and stared in delight.

'Diana! Diana! How did it happen...' She held out her hands to the tall blonde woman who beamed down at her with her gentle sweet smile.

'Veronica, my dear! How lovely to see you. I thought you were on this ship, but I never saw you. What in the world...'

Diana paused, horrified, her greenish-grey eyes startled. Her long slender hand touched the bruise on Veronica's upper arm where the evening wrap of blue silk had slipped back.

'Veronica!' she whispered, her eyes guessing.

Pietro stood to give her his place. Giorgio gave up his chair to her grey-haired plump deaf aunt.

'Diana, you have met Pietro. Pietro, Diana Jansson. She was at our engagement party, and her aunt, Miss Emily Jansson.' Veronica introduced them again happily, beaming at her school friend. 'Oh, Diana, how marvellous! I

73

didn't imagine you could be taking the same ship.'

'We were delayed,' said Diana, sitting down, with a smile at Pietro and his cousin. 'I had planned to sail two weeks ago, but Aunt Emily took sick. We waited and managed to get passage on this one. But you, darling, how are you?' Her look, her murmur, her touch on the bruise were significant. 'I didn't see you anywhere.'

'Oh, I was seasick the first two days,' said Veronica, quickly. 'Then when I went up on deck, alone, I...ah...was dizzy and fell down the steps. Such commotion! Everyone was upset. I wished I had stayed in my cabin! It was most embarrassing!'

Seeing her so happily occupied with her friend, Pietro nodded at her, then left her to speak to an Italian couple on the other side of the lounge. Giorgio was talking with his English friend. Teodosio's gaze had wandered to another Italian couple, he looked at his son, then left the group to join someone he could talk to.

Veronica murmured to Diana, 'Darling, don't look so upset. It wasn't my husband! He saved me! He caught me when I fell.'

Diana looked intensely relieved. 'Oh, darling, I'm so happy! I have heard dreadful stories

74

from other girls. You remember the dreadful French count who married Susan. She was a mass of bruises—and a child a year for two years. She came home and talked to me. Oh, such stories...'

'Oh, Pietro, he just isn't like that! He...he saved me, Diana,' she whispered intensely. 'I think I was *pushed*. I can't talk now but sometime. I am afraid someone is trying to kill me! I mean it.'

Diana went white under her powder and rouge. Her gaze was compassionate, concerned. 'Oh, my dear! Veronica, this is dreadful! Oh, what can I do to help. Let me think...' She bit her lips. 'I was planning to stay in Naples, and paint, then go on to Rome. I know. I'll go only briefly to Naples and Rome, then come directly up to Florence to stay near you. If anything happens I'll be nearby.'

They whispered like conspirators. Diana stopped abruptly when Pietro returned across the room. 'Say nothing,' she muttered. 'Don't trust anyone! I'll be near you on the ship and I'll come to Florence as soon as...' Pietro arrived and stood near them, politely.

Diana stood up. 'Here, I am taking your rightful place,' she said, with her usual sunny friendliness. 'Veronica, we must talk again tomorrow. No more hiding in your cabin. We shall walk on deck, and go ashore at Lisbon...'

Pietro's gaze hardened. 'I am taking Veronica ashore at Lisbon,' he said, rather curtly. 'Perhaps we could meet for tea tomorrow afternoon and discuss this. Giorgio and I have been there many times, and we could escort you and your aunt in our party.'

Diana accepted prettily, with apologies for inviting herself. Veronica was a little sorry that she had. As fond as she was of Diana, she had wanted to be alone with her husband.

The Lisbon expedition was enjoyable, however. The three men escorted the three ladies about in carriages, and pointed out the many places of interest, during the day the ship was in the harbour. That night, they stood on deck and watched the port lights glisten as the ship slid away into the darkness.

'Soon we will be in the Mediterranean and close to our homeland, Italy,' sighed Giorgio, with real satisfaction.

Veronica moved closer to her husband. She suddenly realized she was travelling farther and farther from her own homeland, away from everything she knew and understood, to a strange new land, where she would be completely dependent on her husband and his family.

But Diana would be close by, and Andy Kelly would come within the month, she remembered. She need not be too homesick.

That night, Pietro came to her bed again, but he seemed different. He turned out the lights, and it was dark in the cabin as he came into the bed.

He took her in his arms, and kissed her cheek warmly. 'Did you enjoy today, cara? You are not sick anymore? You seemed to like to walk on the land again.'

'Oh, yes, I felt good,' she sighed, curling against him confidingly. 'To step on the solid earth, it was so good.'

'You will enjoy it when we come to Naples. We will stay there one day, then take the train for Florence. Another time, we can visit Rome. But I want to take you home.'

'Home,' she said. 'That sounds lovely.'

'I hope so much you will love your new home, cara,' he murmured.

He kept on talking, rambling on a little in his deep voice. But she soon lost track of what he was saying, because his hand was moving in a most disturbing fashion on her body. He was moving his palm over the soft cambric of her nightdress, over her rounded breasts, down over her body to her knees and slowly back again.

Moving his hand, kissing her cheek, holding her closer.

She closed her eyes, and pressed her face against his chest. He felt warm and strong, hard under her cheek. So solid, so dependable, so firm against her soft yielding body.

His hand, moving up and down over her body was wakening thrills she had never felt before.

His mouth, moving now to her lips, kissing in soft gentle fashion, then more firmly against her mouth.

His arm, holding her, moving her, turning her to lie against his body.

And his body was so warm, so close, she could feel his solidness against her, and it was strange, suddenly, different, a new body, making her aware of how masculine and hard he was...

Now his hand drew up the nightdress and his palm went slowly over the bare flesh of her thighs. She shivered, and his hand stopped.

'Cara?' he whispered, against her mouth, possessively. 'Cara, cara, cara. I want my wife, I want you.'

She made herself say the words, the words that would start his hand moving on her again, though she would blush for them in the morning light.

'I want you also, Pietro, I do want you.'

His hands were gentle as possible, removing the nightdress, wakening emotions inside her as they stroked over her slim rounded body. She lay on her back, and felt thrill after thrill as he kissed her all over, knowing her, learning her, discovering her secret places. His hands, so careful, so strong, and his mouth, whispering, then kissing, teaching her.

His body, so strong, so hard, yet so gentle. And she knew him that night as she had never known him before. She felt brief pain, so brief that his whispered apology was not necessary. But her mouth kissed him as he whispered, and she held him to her with her arms unexpectedly strong, as he finished the movement.

She sobbed a little in the deep of the bed, sobbed in pleasure, turning her head on the pillow as he moved, blazing with heat and desire.

When it was over, he held her, and they slept for a while. She wakened in the night, still close to him, because the bed was really too small, and he had his arm around her, and his hand on her body.

She lay awake a little while, looking out the window, watching the lights flicker on the ceiling as the waves of the sea glittered and reflected. She had never felt so happy, so complete. Now she was a woman, she thought, and it was a marvellous feeling. To be a woman, to be Pietro's wife.

He wakened as she stirred, and closed his arms strongly about her. 'Veronica,' he said, his voice husky with sleep.

'I am here,' she said softly. He touched her gently, and they came together again.

She wanted to lie awake and be happy, but she could not remain awake for long. The deep strong emotions, the happiness were so tiring, she had to sleep.

All she knew was she was so very very happy. So secure, and safe, and surprised with pleasure. It had been even better, much more beautiful and joyful than Jennie had said.

Pietro left her to sleep late in the morning, while he bathed and had his breakfast on the small deck. When she finally got up and joined him after her bath, he gave her a bright smile of joy and possession.

She had put on her rose-coloured muslin, and a cashmere rose sweater.

'Come here, darling. You are beautiful,' he said. He held out his arms, and she went shyly over to him.

She was drawn down by him onto his lap. He held her and kissed her scarlet cheek. 'You are all right, my cara?' he asked, softly.

She nodded, and leaned her hot face against his shoulder.

'You are so beautiful,' he said again.

She felt a little stab. He hadn't said he loved her. Maybe he did, maybe he didn't. She couldn't ask him. Yet.

But one thing at a time, she thought, as he caressed her, and whispered to her in the warm sunlight, in the gentle swelling lift and fall of the ship on the blue sea. This was so good, she would not ask for more, not now.

As long as she could lie in his arms, feel his kisses, watch the beautiful blue of the Mediterranean sea as it came toward them, as they left the grey angry Atlantic—this was enough for now.

CHAPTER 5

The next several days seemed to spin past in a dizzy whirl of delight for Veronica. The ship stopped again at Gibraltar, and they went ashore, to walk about the fortifications, along the steep streets. She smelled the sweet scents of the exotic gardens, paused at the shop windows, protested in vain as Pietro bought her some souvenirs, some gems, a sweater.

'No, no, I don't need anything. Nothing more, Pietro! Let us find something for Camilla. What would she like?'

'She is easily pleased with anything,' said her elder brother, carelessly, but he seemed to like her thought. They looked over the jewellery, finally chose a pretty enamelled pin and matching pendant set in silver.

Two more days at sea, and then they were in Sicily, in the harbour of Palermo. Pietro and Giorgio were excited about going ashore and exploring. Uncle Teodosio was more wary.

'These Sicilians, you can't trust them,' he kept muttering, not wanting to go ashore at all. He stared glumly at the tall swarthy men who came aboard, their gaudy turbans tying back their black hair. 'Did you lock the cabins firmly, Giorgio? Maybe I will stay in my cabin, they might steal...'

'This is foolish,' said Pietro firmly. 'The stewards will not allow them to come into First Class at all. They will not come near the cabins. Come along, uncle, we must show Palermo to Veronica. We might not return for some years. Come along, don't spoil the fun.'

'Fun, is it, fun?' Teodosio added angrily in Italian. 'You are too much like your father!

Always spending money, always seeking fun! I remember well the time he and I were in Palermo, and he must have his fun, and those Sicilians beat and robbed us, left us for dead, they can't be trusted. You never learn, Pietro!'

'Father, do not say such things,' Giorgio spoke roughly, and looked anxiously at Pietro. The Italian was so rapid that Veronica could scarcely follow it, but she caught the words and translated them.

Pietro had turned pale under his tan, and his eyebrows were drawn and angry. He turned his head from side to side, a sign she was learning meant suffering for him. His dark brown eyes flashed.

'Do you still hold my father's doings against me?' he said, harshly, in Italian. 'Have I not redeemed myself? Must matters be spoken of forever?'

'No, no, of course not,' Teodosio soothed him. He too was drawn and wretched looking. 'But this Sicily, I do not trust these people. It is only that, my boy.'

'It is never enough, though I work, I have married...' Pietro broke off abruptly, gazed anxiously at Veronica. She was gazing at the city of Palermo, gazing beyond the docks, as though she understood nothing of their speech, as though her whole attention was focused on the city.

Her heart was beating painfully. She should have told them she understood their speech. But not now, now when Pietro was saying such things. How could she confess she knew what they were saying.

Her husband went on more quietly, with a hard intensity to his tone. 'I have done everything possible to make up. You hold everything against me personally. You do not approve of anything I have done, yet what else could I have done? This marriage, you did not wish it, yet I must—I must work, it is necessary, you know I have done what must be done...'

She felt choked, suffocated, her husband speaking like this.

Giorgio spoke soothingly, the uncle gave in. 'Yes, yes, we know this, I was only anxious about going ashore in Sicily. It is dangerous...'

'We shall not go if it is truly dangerous,' said Pietro curtly.

The Italian businessman, friend of Teodosio, came up to them. 'What, not going ashore?' he asked, in English, jovially. 'My wife and I are going soon.'

'My uncle believes it is dangerous,' said Pietro, his English strong with the Italian accent. He turned abruptly from the group and leaned with Veronica against the rail, staring

84

down at the dock broodingly.

'Dangerous! Come, Teodosio! You do not mean it...' the businessman said rallyingly. 'This young American lady, she has not seen beautiful Palermo, yes?'

Veronica turned and smiled at him. It was an effort, a terrible effort, because of the pounding of her heart, the whirling of her mind, the guesses she was making.

'No, I have not seen it. Is it truly beautiful?'

'It is very dangerous,' said Teodosio. 'Twenty years ago, when I came with Pietro's father...'

'Twenty years ago! Foolish talk,' said the Italian comfortingly. 'I go ashore with my wife every time I can. We rent a carriage and drive up the hill. Such beautiful views you cannot believe. Come, come, do not be foolish.'

Teodosio allowed himself to be persuaded, and spoke quickly to Pietro in Italian, then in English for Veronica's benefit. 'Well, then, we go ashore. If we must, we must, but I will be on guard.'

Pietro said curtly, in Italian, 'We are always on guard, uncle. You have your knife?'

Veronica shivered as the uncle nodded. Pietro looked at her questioningly.

'It is cool on deck, Pietro,' she murmured.

It was decided they would make a party, the four of them, the Italian businessman and his wife. Pietro went below for Veronica's cloak and a heavier coat for himself...and perhaps a knife, thought Veronica. She did not know what to make of the conversation. Something had happened years before, and Pietro was trying to make up for something his father had done to Pietro's uncle. But how she entered into the matter she could not imagine...except the money, the business.

She had known Pietro did not have much money. There had been a marriage settlement on Pietro, like an Italian dowry. The lawyers had arranged it quietly. But surely, surely, he had not married her—not only for the money!

Or had he?

They took three carriages. They drove about Palermo, and Veronica could almost forget her trouble in the beauty of the city, the glory of its cathedral, the views of the sea from the mountain top. They lingered a long time, until Teodosio became so worried he hurried them back to the city. They ate in a beautiful restaurant. The conversation was more and more in Italian which Veronica pretended not to understand.

In the carriage, she thought, Pietro's arm had often been about her. They were practically alone, and he had pointed out beautiful sights, the flowers, the palm trees, the almond trees.

His voice had been caressing at times. 'You must not fall in love with Palermo,' he had said, as she exclaimed in delight at the glorious tall red flowers. 'I want you to love my Firenze the best.'

'Oh, I shall, Pietro,' she had told him impulsively. 'Your beautiful Florence, that will be my first love...'

'Your *second* love, cara,' he had corrected her, laughing down into her eyes, and had bent and quickly kissed her cheek. 'Your husband demands first place, always, yes? I am a jealous man.'

She hugged the memory of his words now, as they finished their wine, and left the restaurant. No matter why he had married her, he must—he must be coming to love her. He looked at her in such a fond way, he touched her face, her hands often, he praised her beauty, and at night...

At night, he spent the hours in her bed, sometimes making love to her, sometimes holding her so gently, talking in a whisper as though to make their talk more intimate. Even in sleep, he held her close.

They arrived in Naples, and were glad to leave the ship. Giorgio and Teodosio wandered about the city the first evening. Veronica went right to bed. It was marvellous to sleep without being rocked by the constant motion of a ship. And again Pietro was with her all the time.

They spent a full day in Naples, riding about in a carriage. Veronica noted that her husband and his relatives were every bit as alert and wary in Naples as they had been in Palermo. If a ragged man approached their carriage, even to cross the street, every man stiffened, and his hand went to his pocket. She was glad she had three protectors, for some of the ragged men looked so fierce, so dark and savage, it was hard for her to believe they were the civilized Italians, products of twenty centuries of culture.

The following day, they took the train to Florence. The train paused in the railway station in Rome, and she peered curiously from the train windows. It looked immense, this Rome.

'Sometime, we will return to Rome, and visit here. You will enjoy the museums, the concerts, the gardens,' her husband said. 'But I have been away from Florence too long. I am anxious to return and see how the business is going.'

'Of course, there is no hurry,' said Veronica. 'I can see Rome some day, some other time...'

Still she peered and looked and wondered. She was excited by her brief glimpses into her husband's land. She had been reading for two years, studying the language, the culture, the art, the music. There was so much to learn, so much to enjoy.

Even the lazy nonchalant Giorgio was excited about returning to Italy. His voice stumbled over English words as he spoke to her. 'You must see the fine hotels in Rome, Veronica. You must visit the concert halls, the finest opera in Europe—'

'No, no, Milan, that is much better,' Teodosio protested.

'Rome has the best singers now!' his son argued. 'And Veronica must visit the galleries of art—Rome has the best.'

'We have the best in Florence,' said Pietro. His eyes twinkled humorously at Veronica as they argued in English. She smiled back at him.

'No, no, how can you say that? We have little compared with Rome,' Giorgio went on passionately, unusually aroused. 'The artists here, they work so hard, they live on bread and spaghetti in order to work, how they work at their art...' His hands sketched in the air, with intensity. 'All, all for their art.'

Veronica looked at him in some surprise. She had not thought Giorgio could get intense about

89

anything at all. So he loved art, did he? She wondered if he had tried to be an artist, but had been persuaded not to try anything so contrary to his heritage as a member of a royal family. She knew Uncle Teodosio now enough to know he looked down on Pietro and on her father for being in trade.

She too grew excited as the train approached Florence. Pietro pointed out places to her, named names she would not remember, in growing pleasure at their return. Giorgio was beaming from the train at the very countryside, at the tall dark cypresses, the trim green lawns, the green bushes, the glimpses of castles on the hillsides, the more frequent houses, the roads, donkey carts, riders on horseback.

'Now, now we grow near,' said Uncle Teodosio.

'It is a half an hour yet,' said Pietro.

'That is closer than two months,' said his uncle drily.

Uncle Teodosio spoke the truth for all of them, Veronica thought. It must have been hard for these home-loving Italian men to be away from their beloved Florence for so long, waiting for the engagement, the marriage, all the ceremonies.

Finally they arrived in the station in Florence, and were met by their own carriage.

The servants beamed at Pietro and his uncle and cousin, stared frankly, wide-eyed at blonde Veronica, led them to the carriage outside. The luggage would follow in a second carriage, Pietro said. 'Oh, oh, oh,' said Veronica, again and again, as the open carriage started through the streets of Florence. 'There is the cathedral, the baptistery, the...oh, the tower of Giotto. Oh, how beautiful, how lovely.'

The sun was going down, glimmering rosy over the cream and beige and red and gold of the city buildings. The Giotto tower turned rosy, shimmering like a sea shell in the evening light. Lights twinkled from restaurants, from coffee shops. It was warmer than Veronica had expected, and she shrugged back her heavy cloak. October. October in Florence, Italy, and the air was sweet with strange scents—coffee, flowers, spices, she could not name them all.

'Ah, I'm coming down to Florence tomorrow,' sighed Giorgio. 'I have not seen my friends for too many months.'

'And you have much to brag about,' said Teodosio, and they all laughed. 'I expect you will mention the blonde English girl...merely in passing, eh?'

Veronica wanted to laugh also, then realized she was not supposed to understand their Italian. She grew more and more uncomfortable each day that she did not confess.

Now the carriage had left the centre of the city, travelled briskly into the streets filled with houses, tall strange houses, some bulky as fortresses, stone-built, sturdy, as though they had stood for hundreds of years.

Then as the carriage moved on, they came to newer houses. On up the hillside they went, out into the countryside, past large villas set back from the road. She glimpsed views as the carriage wound round and round the long road uphill, views down into the city of Florence, where the sunset was gleaming on the fairytale city, glancing off the rooves, glowing off the buildings, the towers, the steeples. Bells were ringing, and their chimes clashed, harmonized, rang out again and again, a thin sweetness on the air, gentled by distance. All Florence seemed bathed in a pink glow, alive with bells and light.

Veronica leaned back into Pietro's ready arm. 'It is so beautiful, like a marvellous story,' she whispered. 'I love it already.'

He pressed his cheek quickly to hers. 'I am glad, cara. I want you to love it as I do.'

The horses were straining as they pulled the carriage uphill, farther up and up. Florence was still visible, but farther away. She looked up, up, into the hillside.

'At the top is Fiesole, but we live only halfway to the top,' Pietro said. 'Sometime we will drive up and see the ruins there, also the cathedral. There is a church there with a beautiful Della Robbia madonna. You will adore her, with her strange blue colours, her gleaming white...'

'Almost home,' said Teodosio, twisting around. They were coming to a high stone wall, now a thick iron fence. Someone ran from inside the grounds to open the fence. Pietro waved. The man shouted a welcome in Italian, excitedly.

'Ah—home,' murmured Giorgio.

Veronica gasped. As they drove inside the gates, she could see the Villa d'Oro. It glowed in the last rays of the setting sun, like a topaz in its enamelled green setting. Just as Pietro had told her. The pale golden villa took on the rosy hue of the sunset, and gleamed back in gold to them. The windows long and slender glittered with the sun. It was huge, she thought, and so beautiful, so glamorous, like the castle of a fairy princess...

Tall cypresses lined the drive, all tall and elegant and dark, almost black instead of their true green colour. The horses quickened their pace, on the level now, and scenting home and rest. The driver turned into the gravelled way

93

in front of the villa. The wide doors were opened, several people stood there, calling to them.

Pietro helped Veronica out of the carriage as
soon as it had halted. A tall girl ran forward,
hugged Pietro, turned to Veronica. Veronica
looked into her face, and thought, I know her,
I have seen her before...where?

The girl smiled, hesitated, then impulsively
reached out her arms. Veronica found herself
folded into a tight embrace, the girl murmuring in English, a little broken, 'Welcome,
welcome, my sister!' The girl kissed her on
her cheek.

'Camilla,' said Veronica. 'How sweet of you,
thank you.' She almost shuddered with the
relief of this welcome, so different from what
she had anticipated. A jealous sister, cold,
haughty.

But this girl was sweet, gentle, affectionate,
welcoming.

She drew Veronica to the house. Veronica
moved into her new home with her new sister
on one arm, her new husband holding her on
the other side. She felt warmed, welcomed, at
home.

They drew her inside, past lines of servants,
maids beaming, stately men in livery staring
curiously at her blonde hair as the cloak had
slipped back.

They led her into a large living room. 'I will show you your rooms later. You must be so... ver' hungry,' said Camilla. 'Oh, do I speak bad? I try to learn much English ver-ree fast,' she said, blushing, looking anxious.

'You speak marvellously,' said Veronica. 'Oh, have I met you? You look so familiar. Pietro, I haven't met her...or maybe you look like Pietro...' Puzzled, dazzled by the bright lights of the huge living room, she looked from her husband to her new sister. The face was so familiar, the sweet oval face, the large brown eyes with the well-defined eyebrows, the dimpled chin, the waving brown hair. She frowned, puzzled.

Giorgio laughed, even Pietro laughed happily. Camilla was blushing.

'You stop it,' she ordered her men imperiously. 'It is not the joke! Stop it. I explain,' she said, to Veronica. 'It is silly, really. They say I look like the Botticelli models.'

'She does,' said Pietro, hugging her affectionately. 'She could step right into a painting. You see this face—like a Botticelli angel. Only the temper does not match!'

Camilla punched her brother in the ribs. Veronica stared at her in surprise, at the lovely face, the slim hands, the sensitive expression. Yes, she did look like a Botticelli angel, or one of the goddesses, a true Florentine such as Botticelli had painted. She was truly beautiful.

'Now, we ignore those foolish men,' said Camilla. 'Come, you will be so hungry. We have the food, the wine ready—come, my sister.' She took her in her arm as possessively as her brother, and led her off to the dining room. She scolded her brother, her uncle, her cousin with one breath, turned and spoke affectionately to Veronica in the next, ordered the maids in a third, all so rapidly that Veronica was dazed.

Hot food was brought. Veronica was seated at the head of the table, at the other end her husband. Camilla had happily given her the place as head of the household, she realized, as the servants turned to her for orders. Camilla poured some white wine for her, asked anxiously for her to try it.

'I like it best. It is not so—how you say—so strong as the red ones that the men enjoy. I like this one. Please, you try this?'

Veronica tried it, found it mild, sweet, with a slight tang to her tongue. She praised it, and Camilla reacted with as much relief as though someone's life had depended on it.

'Tomorrow, I show you around the house, the gardens, introduce all the servants. Tomorrow, I will...' she was rattling on when

Pietro interrupted from the other end of the long polished table.

'Tomorrow, my wife will rest, Camilla! She has had a long journey. And I don't want you running down to Florence with her the first week! I will take her when I am ready. You will wear her out. I warn you, Veronica, this little one is too full of energy and plans. Do not let her drag you here and there.' He was smiling, though, with affection at his lively sister.

Camilla turned impulsively to Veronica, and pressed her hand with her own warm slim hand. 'I will not hurt you for anything. Never! No, no. You must rest tomorrow. Yes? When you are ready, we run around good.'

Veronica laughed happily. She had found a friend, a girl friend who was bubbling with enthusiasm, eager for affection, a girl as open and sweet as one could wish.

She felt very happy, though weary, when Camilla showed them up to their new rooms. In their absence, the girl had prepared the master suite of rooms, four huge rooms at one side of the villa, overlooking the gardens, and a magnificent view of Florence down in the valley.

Long French windows opened onto the stone balcony. The huge drapes were of white edged

97

with blue in Veronica's massive bedroom, large enough to run around and around for morning exercises, the girl thought, dazed at its immensity. The walls were covered with a delicate blue and white design. The ceilings were gilded, decorated with cupids and goddesses, and little imps peeping with laughing eyes from the corners, all gold and white.

Pietro's room was next to hers, equally massive, with red drapes and red and gold decorations. They shared a huge bathroom, gleaming white, again with a gold decorated ceiling. Their living room was beyond Pietro's room. Veronica just glanced at it. It was too big to take in at once, but she got the impression of blue and white and red roses and red velvet, small exquisite tables of wood, a huge table covered with a design in mosaic.

'Does it please you?' Camilla was asking anxiously, but looking toward her brother. Her slim hands twisted together.

'Oh, it is the most beautiful place I have ever seen, the most beautiful rooms, the loveliest...' Veronica paused. She could not express her pleasure in words. She hugged Camilla. 'Thank you, thank you, dear sister!'

Camilla hugged her back, looking over her shoulder at her brother, waiting for his words.

'It is well done,' he said firmly. 'Just as I

asked. We are pleased, dear Camilla.'

Camilla relaxed with a great sigh of relief. Veronica realized then the burden it must have been for Pietro's younger sister, only seventeen.

Veronica felt very weary now. Pietro sent the bubbling Camilla away, and Veronica went to bed. Pietro came and sat on the edge of her bed, after she was safely tucked in.

'You are most tired, cara,' he said. 'I leave you to sleep alone. Eh? But if you get lonely, you come to my room. There is always room for you in my big bed. Better than the ship, yes? I think you need much sleep. You will sleep late tomorrow.'

He touched her cheek with his warm palm, then bent and kissed her on the mouth. She put her arms around his neck, and kissed him back. 'Thank you, Pietro, for everything—'

She slept hard that night, slept long. When she wakened, the sun was high in the sky. She could not think where she was for a moment, then she saw a laughing imp peeping at her from the ceiling. She laughed back at him. Now she remembered.

She got up, bathed, and dressed. It must be late. She saw a gold and white clock on one table, almost noon! She rang the long cord for a maid, and the middle-aged woman appeared like magic.

'Coffee,' said the maid, and laid a tray on one of the tables. She drew up a chair, beamed, indicated Veronica should sit down. In Italian, she rattled off, 'Lunch will be served in the dining room at one o'clock.'

A tall man in livery came in the opened door, carrying two suitcases. In Italian, he said, 'Maddalena, stupid, you are silly. She doesn't talk Italian. Tell the mistress to come up and speak to her.'

Maddalena looked downcast. Veronica almost said to her in Italian that she understood.

'She is very lovely,' said Maddalena. 'One can understand why the master married such a beauty. Look at that gold hair.'

'He probably looked at her gold purse,' said the man, crudely. He thumped down the bags.

'You be careful,' said Maddalena. 'You gossip stupidly. And have a care of her cases!'

'They are as heavy as though they had money in them. Well, this house will be the richer for it. But he should have married a good Italian girl,' said the man.

Veronica was seated at her coffee. She kept her eyes down, so the rage and humiliation would not show.

Two other men in livery came in with her trunk. They moved it carefully to avoid scratching the beautiful wood panelling of the door. Maddalena directed them, bossily, to set it in one corner. She pointed at it, looked at Veronica. 'Keys?' she asked, in Italian.

Veronica looked at her, at the trunk, then silently rose and obtained her purse. She handed her keys to the maid, who beamed in satisfaction at being understood.

'There, she understands me,' said the maid, triumphantly to the men.' Her wrinkled face crinkled up in smiles. Her grey hair fell about her face, from the mob cap, as she bent to open the trunk.

'Just try to follow her orders, silly,' said the first man, crossly. 'You won't understand each other then! She is one of those American women, and they are impossible! They demand, demand, and let the master find that out soon! If she wasn't rich, he might have listened to his uncle! But no, he has to marry a rich girl, he tells his uncle. Giorgio himself, he warned Pietro.'

'You talk too much of other's affairs,' said Maddalena severely. 'Go. Don't gossip so much.'

The men shrugged and left. Veronica sat long over her coffee, and it seemed bitter to her. The maid chatted to herself, murmuring over the dresses as she took them out.

She was here, alone, in a strange country. She was married, subject to her husband. The husband who had married her because she was rich!

She knew it was the truth, she had known it all along. If she had been poor, he would never have looked at her. They would never even have met. It was a marriage of her money and his titles. She had known that.

But hearing the words from the blunt voices of servants had given her a shock. Giorgio and Uncle Teodosio had warned Pietro, they had been cool and aloof, though correct in their behaviour to her. They hadn't wanted the marriage either.

Only Camilla had been cordial to her. And that, Veronica began to realize, was because she wished to please her brother.

When Camilla came to her room later, Veronica wanted to be cold and distant also, she felt so hurt. But no one could resist the warmth and sweetness of the lovely girl, and Veronica wanted a friend very badly in this household.

CHAPTER 6

Veronica was doubly delighted to see Andy Kelly on his return to Florence. She wanted a friend near her. And she was anxious to hear his report. Perhaps he would calm and end forever her fears about her father's death.

They had lunch with the family. After the meal, Pietro, Veronica, Camilla and Andy retired to the yellow salon. He praised it.

'This is so bright, so pretty. One feels happy here,' he added, in Italian, to Camilla. 'Did you help design this? I think someone of a happy nature designed it.'

She blushed prettily, in pleasure and surprise. 'Oh, thank you. I did. But you speak Italian! How wonderful!'

Veronica looked quickly from one to the other of them. She said nothing.

Pietro said, heavily, 'Speak in English, please. This is rude to my wife, Camilla!'

She blushed like a red rose, and hung her head like a child.

Veronica spoke now, hurt for Camilla. 'I do understand Italian, a little,' she added hastily.

'I have been studying by myself. Perhaps Camilla will help me improve, so I can speak it well before long. It is awkward for everyone to have to speak English just for me. I must learn to be able to order the servants also.'

Pietro seemed to melt. 'You have been learning? But this is marvellous. Of course Camilla will help you. Or we can hire a tutor for you. Just as you please. Tutoring would help you improve rapidly.'

'That would be fine. We will consider this,' said Veronica, with relief. She felt she had gotten something heavy off her conscience.

Pietro, Veronica and Andy settled down around a large table. Camilla sat nearby, listening, more as a companion than as one concerned.

Andy spread out his designs, then emptied a packet of gems from a small leather pouch. Veronica exclaimed in delight at the gems, touching them with small expert fingers.

'These are from the New York office. They wished us to set them here in Florence, in the new flower designs,' Andy explained. 'Perhaps a butterfly with the garnets in a gold setting. We have orders we cannot fill yet for the ladies this winter in New York,' Andy boasted to Pietro, with satisfaction. 'The rage is all for flowers, butterflies, golden bees, items from nature which are small and delicate.'

Veronica looked through his designs, picked out one of a spray of flowers visited by a small golden bee. 'This one—this is exquisite. I see it as a hair-piece, just in the front, set on a small comb.'

They studied the designs, talked about the gems, about the orders. Pietro contributed some suggestions. Camilla seemed interested, and jumped up several times to look over their shoulders at the designs and gems, as Andy laid them out with tweezers over the papers.

'Pietro and I have been designing some new things also,' said Veronica, remembering. She stood up, to get them.

'You mean, my dear, that you have had some ideas, and I have been enchanted with them,' her husband corrected firmly, in his strong masculine voice, though smiling at her.

Veronica sent him a shy delighted smile over her shoulder, her blonde curls moving with her head-turning. She bent over a small table at the side of the room, opened the drawer, took out some sketches. She sifted through them, hesitated.

'Show him all of them,' Pietro suggested. 'You have some marvellous ideas. Another opinion on them would be good.'

'But you liked best the ones with the rubies

105

and diamonds,' she objected, biting her lip thoughtfully.

'Nevertheless, I am only one man. Another designer's ideas would be good. Show him all, Veronica.'

She obeyed him at once, and brought the entire sheaf of drawings back to the table. Camilla was yawning, daintily.

Veronica murmured to her, 'Perhaps you would like to take a nap, darling. You usually have a siesta. This will only bore you.'

Pietro was glancing at his watch. 'And I have seen the designs. I will be glad to have your decisions, but I feel you two should reach a conclusion. I am only the shop manager, after all.'

'Oh, Pietro, you must have a say in this, of course!' Veronica protested, distressed.

He reached out, touched her cheek with one finger, in the way she loved. 'You are the artist, cara,' he said, softly. 'And I must go and see about the gardens. Camilla was very distressed at what the new man is doing to the roses. I shall return presently.'

He left the room, and Camilla excused herself, still yawning like a sleepy child. Veronica and Andy were left alone, though the door to the golden salon was wide open.

He began looking over her sheaf of designs.

He sighed deeply as he looked at one sketch after another.

'What is wrong, Andy? Tell me, don't spare my feelings,' she said, anxiously, as he finished. 'You don't like them. You know what is wanted in the market. These are bad, aren't they?'

'No, Veronica, they are not bad. They are good, extraordinarily good,' he said, with another big sigh. He laughed a little. 'Don't look like that, boss-lady,' he teased. 'I am jealous of you, that is all. You have inherited your father's taste and flair. These have my designs beaten easily. I would like to throw mine in the fire!'

'No, no, don't,' she said, laughing, and caught at his wrist, as he would have gathered up his own sketches threateningly. 'Don't tease, Andy. I hope my designs can be used, but I am under no illusions...'

He turned serious at the touch of her hand. 'Listen, Veronica, let's forget the designs a minute. I have to tell you,' he said in a rapid low tone. 'About your father...'

She felt as though the blood were draining from her body. The moment she had feared was here. 'Andy, what did you...did you find...'

He nodded. He looked half-sick, his skin

paling. 'I can't tell you what we did, it was very nasty. My father scolded us. But it had to be done. Veronica, my medical friend found arsenic in the body, so much that it had to be the cause of death.'

'Arsenic!' she muttered. She put her hand to her throat. The rapid pulse beat was choking her. 'Arsenic. Who...then...who...'

'Who else but the doctor who had charge of him all those months?' asked Andy. 'The servants might have helped.'

'Oh, no, not the servants! They adored him, Jennie, all of them. They cried when he died. Oh, Andy, they would not have done this!'

'Sybil, then, your stepmother. She wants to marry the doctor, Dr Heinrich.' The words hung heavily between them.

'But on the ship,' she whispered. 'Sybil wasn't on the ship. The doctor wasn't there!'

'What happened on the ship?' he asked sharply.

She sighed, trembled. She finally forced the words. 'I was seasick. When I finally went up on deck alone, Pietro was playing a game with some men. I was on an upper deck, looking down. I was pushed, hard, from behind. I fell down the stairs. Pietro caught me.'

She was shaking so hard he put his hands on hers to calm her. Her hands felt cold as ice.

'Poor darling. Tell me. Who pushed you?'

'I don't know. I saw a form, tall, a man in a black cloak. Pietro saw him also, heard me scream. Someone said...said that if I had fallen through the railing which had opened...I would have gone right into the sea. It was stormy, no one could have rescued me.'

'My God, my God,' he whispered. 'And Sybil...she wasn't on board. I saw her in New York the week after you sailed.'

'Where did you see her?' she asked sharply. 'Did you go to the house? Was Dr Heinrich there?'

'No, I was in my father's office. We planned to take the train to the country together after work on Friday. Sybil was there, arguing. She wanted to break the will. She argued that she deserved half of his estate. And most of the estate was in this jewellery business. She said that it wasn't fair you should have all of it.'

'I don't know why father made the will like that. She was never interested in the business, though. Maybe he thought she would sell it.'

'But you are in danger of being killed,' he said bluntly. 'Veronica, you must be very very careful. If you are in danger, here in this villa...'

'Of course I am not,' she interrupted angrily.

'My husband, his family, they would never harm me!'

'I'm not saying they would. But be careful!'

'I am safe, now I'm in Florence,' she repeated stubbornly. Her shaking hands shifted through the drawings. 'Andy, let's go back to the designs. Please don't speak of this again. I'm grateful you found out, but there is nothing I can do now about my father, except to carry on his work.'

They chatted away about the designs, and he marked their decisions on the design slips, diamonds here, garnets there, set in gold, set in silver, a golden bee sipping a ruby flower, a spray swaying almost visibly under the weight of a delicate butterfly.

They worked much of the afternoon on the designs. Veronica ordered tea at four, saying, 'Camilla will soon be down to join us. She loves tea. We will have coffee for Pietro.'

Until the tea arrived, Andy and Veronica kept on with their work, heads together, busily marking the designs.

'No, no, we must have that one in emeralds,' she insisted, as he began to mark one for a cheaper stone. 'I think it will sell in emeralds.'

'You may be right. But it will sell faster in this way, so what do you want? You're the boss,' he teased, laughing. 'You give the

110

orders, boss. I just carry them out.'

'No, you are the chief designer for Florence, now,' she said. 'It has to be your final decision. But I do like that emerald stone you brought.'

He picked up the stone and set it on the finger of a hand nearest him. Smiling, he said, 'I'd make a ring for you, if you would let me. Look how lovely this is on your hand.'

'It is beautiful.' She admired it, her blonde head very close to his, as the lights were growing dark in the gay yellow salon.

'What, you are still working?' Pietro's deep voice echoed through the room as he strode in from the garden through the French doors. He blinked at them, stared incredulously as they sprang apart guiltily. 'What is this?' he asked, in Italian.

'We were trying the emerald on her hand,' said Andy, flushing red.

'I have ordered tea. Camilla will be down soon,' said Veronica, jumping up. She was both distressed and angry that she should have appeared in such a compromising light.

Pietro turned cold and hard right before her gaze. 'Is she still asleep? I thought she would be awake long ago, or I should have returned at once,' he said, significantly, staring at them angrily.

111

Camilla came in the door from the hallway. 'They say Andy's carriage has been waiting for an hour,' she said. 'Is he still...oh, there you are,' she said, her eyes wide at them.

Veronica had never felt more guilty in her life. And she was so innocent, she thought.

'I really must go,' said Andy curtly. 'It is late. I ought to get back to Florence before dark...'

'The servants are bringing tea,' said Veronica, in her husband's direction. She refused to be convicted without a trial.

He glared at her, his dark eyes cold. She drooped her head, and touched the sketches with a shaking hand. No. The judge had passed sentence. She would not be given a chance to defend herself.

Andy scooped the gems into the leather pouch, gathered up all the sketches. 'I'll take these down to Florence with me this evening, and go over them.'

'Fine,' Pietro cut in, as Andy would have continued. 'I'll look at them in the shop tomorrow, and we can go ahead with the more practical ones.'

Veronica flinched at the sneer in his tone. She and Camilla accompanied Andy to the door, and their farewells were short.

Veronica felt horrible about it, and indignant

at the same time. She had done nothing wrong. It was Pietro, a typical Italian, unreasonably jealous, impossible, cold and rude and haughty at nothing. Rude to a man because he was an American, without a title, one who worked for his living instead of marrying money, Veronica thought angrily, then was ashamed again.

When she returned to the yellow salon, it was empty. Pietro had left the villa, and she did not see him again that night.

CHAPTER 7

The next few days seemed impossible for Veronica. Pietro was cold and distant to her. Camilla fluttered between them, a messenger of peace, a distressed butterfly.

Veronica would not apologize for anything she had done. She thought angrily, he is just jealous of my work. He is angry because another man looked at me. He is unreasonable. I would not betray him. I am not a flirt.

She was as cold to him, though it hurt her to be like that. Giorgio and Teodosio seemed to sense what was wrong, and it amused and touched her that they were anxious about it.

She was stretched out on a lounge chair in the terrace below the house one afternoon. The late October sunshine flickered over the last of the roses, the trim green bushes, the dolphin fountain that shone wetly under its showers. She felt lazy and tired, though she had done little for a week except sketch and supervise the housekeeping. Camilla did much of the latter.

Giorgio came strolling from the bottom of the gardens, from the greenhouse where the plants were kept in winter. He saw her stretched out, paused for a visible moment, then came toward her.

'Cousin Veronica, may I join you for a little while?' he asked, pausing at a chair near her.

'Of course, Giorgio. And please...' she added boldly, 'please speak in Italian, slowly. I am beginning to understand it, you know. I need to practice.'

He beamed at her, unexpectedly. 'That is magnificent,' he said, in Italian. 'So you catch on to us, quickly, eh? Good, good. I speak slowly for you.' He seated himself, gazed at her quickly, then down at his big hands. He was like Pietro in many ways, his darkness, his strength, his bigness. Only Pietro seemed driven by the need to work, whereas Giorgio seemed lazy and languid to Veronica.

She leaned her head back on the cushions

114

and closed her eyes. She wondered if she needed a tonic. She felt so tired. Maybe it was the air, so clear, so pure, high above the city.

'Veronica, I am troubled. We are all troubled,' Giorgio finally went on, in Italian. 'Here you are, a lovely bride, and Pietro and you are angry at each other. You have both too much temper, perhaps? Excuse me, I am a boor and a fool. But I am troubled for you. Such a beautiful couple, only one month married, and you are fighting. This is terrible, this is dreadful.'

She had to smile at his dramatic tone. He dearly loved his operas, she thought, even away from the theatre!

'All married couples have their troubles, Giorgio,' she told him, choosing her words with care. The Italian came more easily now, that she had been talking to Camilla for a week, and to the servants. She was glad the deception was over, that they now knew that she could understand their language to a certain extent. 'We are from different countries. Pietro believes I am too free and bold. But I am an American woman...'

'You are Italian, now,' he corrected her quickly.

She flushed, and sat up straight. 'I am still an American!' she told him curtly. 'I love Italy,

115

but I am still an American!' She glared at him.

He shook his dark handsome head ruefully. 'So, I start another quarrel. Bad Giorgio. I mean to smooth the waters, not rouse them up. Stupid man. I try again. Veronica, dear, Pietro is a very jealous man. Perhaps I tell something —a secret that is not a secret—to let you understand him.'

She wasn't sure whether to encourage him, but her curiosity was aroused. Pietro rarely spoke of himself or his past. 'Go on, Giorgio, please.' She leaned back again wearily in the comfortable lounge chair.

'The father of Pietro,' Giorgio began slowly, 'was a fine man, the older brother of my father. Only the two men were of the family. Uncle had charge of the family fortune, he invested all the monies of the family—you understand? I don't talk too quickly? Good, I continue. Pietro was engaged to a lovely beauty, an Italian loveliness...' He kissed his fingers dramatically. 'Of such a beauty! This Regina Ruggeri is of the finest families, of money, gracious, of royal birth, equal to us. The families approved. Then, misfortune. The politics of my sad country—you have read, yes? The fortunes were swept away overnight. All of ours, I should say most of ours, and much of the Ruggeri family.'

'Oh, I didn't know...' Veronica breathed softly. A beauty, Regina, of royal birth. Was this the girl they thought should have married Pietro? Her curiosity was strong. 'What did this Regina Ruggeri look like?'

'A raven-haired beauty,' said Giorgio dreamily. 'Large dark eyes, like bits of the midnight sky, a skin of cream, a laugh of bird-song..'

Raven-haired. Veronica touched the long blonde curl hanging over her shoulder. She wondered if Pietro regretted his raven-haired beauty. Probably.

'To continue,' said Giorgio, his dark eyes flashing dramatically. How the Italians loved a sad story, she thought. 'The money—gone! Pietro scarcely twenty-one. His father ill with worry, finally he died. The engagement was postponed, again, again. How we wept, together, over the worry! The palazzo in Florence was sold, we wept bitterly over every stone.'

The palazzo in Florence—she had not known there had been one. She scarcely breathed, hoping that Giorgio would not be interrupted. She was learning more about Pietro than he had ever told her.

Giorgio continued, his hands flashing in the air, his black eyes snapping, shadowed, widening, his head turning with all the airs of an

117

opera singer. She would have been amused if she hadn't been so intent on understanding what he said. The further he got into his story, the more rapidly his words snapped and sizzled.

'The palazzo on the Golden Isle—it has been closed. Pietro could not bear to sell it, so all the servants were discharged. Such weeping, you could not bear it. The Palazzo, the golden palazzo for us, the palazzo of the Duke d'Isola d'Oro was closed forever. Pietro asked Regina to wait for him, she promised, swearing to wait. He went to America, he met your father, he learned the business of the jewellery, he went into trade. We could have managed without this, but Pietro, he was determined not to live on the money of the Ruggeri.' Giorgio paused, sighed, wiped his hands over his face.

'And then, he returned to Florence...' Veronica prompted, in a low tone.

'Yes. In less than one year, he returned, with success in his hands.' Giorgio held out his own hands dramatically. 'But the raven-beauty, she had fled. She had been married by her family to a rich man, a man old enough to be her grandfather. Pietro swore he would kill. He went to see Regina. He returned, so white you would have wept for him. She was happy, he said, she was wearing such jewels you couldn't believe. She wore gowns of richest silk, embroidered with pearls. She told him he could remain her lover.' Giorgio's voice lowered to a whisper, his eyes wide. 'That man—he told her to go to hell! Yes, Pietro told her this. He worked, how he worked. He was so mad! Then years later, we have the happy ending,' he leaned back smiling. 'He goes to America on another business trip, he meets the golden-haired princess of his dreams, he marries her, he brings her back to Italy. All is happy again, yes?'

Veronica wished she could say yes so firmly. She smoothed the pink muslin gown. A silk gown, embroidered with pearls. She felt rather sick.

'So he married you,' said Giorgio, anxiously, prompting her. She wasn't responding with an aria of happiness, the way the opera singer would have.

'But I heard she is a widow,' said Veronica, dully. 'He could have married her, if he had waited.'

Giorgio shrugged expressively, widely. 'He didn't want to! His temper, it is of a firmness! He hates her, he despises her. You will see this Italian beauty when you go to the Pergola concert on Saturday, you will see her. Such a beauty, and free to marry him, but he chose *you*.

You see, he adores you.'

Veronica wished she could be so sure. Did Pietro adore her? Or was he merely performing his conjugal duties perfectly? She did not know. All she knew was that her heart ached for him, even when she was furious with him.

'You will mend this little quarrel?' asked Giorgio. 'You will be discreet with the American man, so Pietro will not have his jealousy aroused once more? You see, he is so sensitive—'

Camilla came out of the villa, down the wide steps toward them. Giorgio sighed, stood up for her, looked down at Veronica anxiously. She avoided his gaze.

'Did you have a good sleep?' asked Camilla. 'The roses are more beautiful now. Let me pick one yellow rose for you, cara,' she said, and bending over the bushes, she carefully chose the most perfect one and snapped it off.

Veronica accepted it with a smile. They were trying so hard to please her, but the one she cared most about was avoiding her. Was it her fault? Should she be docile and submissive, and hide in her room when Andy came? She had to see him on business. She should go down to Florence again soon, and consult with him, but Pietro had flared up angrily at the idea. She would have to wait until he could accompany her, he had said.

And they had quarrelled, briefly, but violently.

Pietro had been gone three days, a visit to Rome on business. She had been sorely tempted to order the carriage and go down to Florence, and defy him. Something had held her back.

He returned that evening, weary, but triumphant. He told her, in the yellow salon, 'The shop has orders for dozens of pieces from Rome. The contessas are so very pleased with the new designs, everyone must have a specially designed piece of the house of Murray in Florence. Does that please you?'

'Oh, Pietro, it is marvellous!' she cried, her anger forgotten. 'How successful you are! We must set to work at once. You have the details I asked for? Each lady's height and colour of hair?'

'Yes, yes, I have them all.' He grimaced ruefully. He drew out papers from his pockets. 'You would have laughed to see me study the ladies attentively, and scribbling down their heights and colours! Two ladies asked me what I did, and I told them what you had said. So they wished to come to Florence, and see you, have you design for them alone! I could not persuade them against this. They wish to come

121

next month. Two contessas.'

'Oh, a triumph!' cried Camilla, happily. 'Veronica, this is marvellous. We will celebrate tonight! There shall be special wines brought up for dinner.'

Pietro was so happy over his orders, which would keep the shop busy for months, that he seemed to have forgotten his anger and jealousy. She was glad about that, she had wanted to patch things over without admitting she had been seriously at fault.

Pietro had already arranged for her to attend a concert with him on Saturday afternoon at the Pergola in Florence. The next day—after a night of sleeping alone, for he had kept to his own room—she approached him after breakfast.

'Pietro, on Saturday, could we go to Florence early? I do need to consult with Andy Kelly on the designs. And I want to go shopping with you,' she added hastily, as a cloud gathered on his face. 'I want a new gown of rose silk, I have determined to have one. Did you know your wife was so frivolous?' She gazed up at him from under her long lashes, half-teasingly.

He seemed to melt from his growing anger. 'Cara, cara, don't you have a dozen new gowns? Very well, you must have another. There is a fine shop near ours, I shall take you

122

there and introduce you. I will take our new orders to Andy Kelly also.'

So they made a peace of sorts, and the whole household seemed to relax and breathe more easily. Giorgio returned to his lazy self-contained ways, and watched them approvingly from a distance. He probably thought he had smoothed over everything, Veronica thought with some amusement. Well, he had helped, to her surprise. He did have a kind heart, well-hidden.

Camilla looked wistful when they mentioned the concert. Veronica looked at her husband, and he promised to get tickets for them all the next time. 'But this is a Beethoven concert, cara Camilla,' he said firmly. 'You do not like him enough yet.'

'How can I learn to like him if I don't hear him?' she asked, the first sign of rebellion Veronica remembered in her.

Giorgio interrupted. 'Camilla, foolish one, they wish to be alone! Now, do not interfere! Besides, we shall all go to the opera as soon as it starts next month. You know how much you love the opera.'

She grew radiant again. 'Oh, yes, yes, we shall go to the opera. You love opera, don't you, Veronica? You must love it.'

The Saturday expedition was a perfect one

to begin. The day was a beautiful sunny one, with a slight cool breeze, as their carriage drove swiftly down the steep hills and slopes to Florence in the valley below. A blue haze hung over the steeples at first, then lifted slowly, as the sun burned it away. How the rooves glowed, how the cream and gold and burnt brown shone in the sunshine. The sky was like the Italian paintings of sky—a vivid blue of Madonna colours, and fleecy white clouds drifting in it, rolling over the hills, lifting to show the glorious greens and browns and golden colours of the city and countryside.

'Oh, how beautiful it is,' Veronica murmured, catching at Pietro's hand impulsively. 'I could not bear to live anywhere else. It is as beautiful as you said, even more so. It catches at the heart, and will not let go. In the evening, I lay on the terrace, and heard the bells chiming from Florence, so like angel bells...'

He lifted her hand to his lips. 'And did you miss me, cara? Even with all the beauty around you?'

He was half-laughing, half-serious. 'Yes, I missed you,' she admitted shyly. Then impulsively, 'Pietro, I am so sorry I quarrelled with you. I will be a good wife, I promise. I will never deceive you with any man, ever! It

124

hurt me to think you believed that...' She gazed up at him anxiously.

His face had closed up somewhat, but he squeezed her hand reassuringly. 'It is all right, cara, I told you I am a jealous man. There is much to adjust between us. I knew it would not be easy,' he added, half to himself.

So it was settled, and she felt much happier. In Florence, he took her first to the silk store, where she raved over the glorious brocades, silks, velvets. She could not decide over the material for a new gown, so Pietro finally decided for her.

'We will have this rose brocade, made up in the second design, signora,' he said firmly to the woman. 'And a blue velvet, this one, of the softest blue, in a full design, not too low cut, but low enough to show off the collar of pearls. And a golden silk—this one here—just lighter than the hair of my signora. There, Veronica, will that satisfy you for a month or two?' He laughed down at her teasingly.

'Oh, not three gowns, Pietro! One is enough...'

But he overrode her protests firmly, and they went on to the Murray shop in the next block.

There was a little awkwardness at first, as Andy greeted them. Veronica had not seen him since Pietro had sent him angrily on his way.

But the other designers came around, and looked at the table spread with designs, and listened to her instructions. Pietro explained the Rome orders, and there was much murmuring and gasping at the size and high cost of the orders.

'We'll make up your emeralds the way you said, Veronica,' said Andy, excitedly. 'There must be much more of a market than we ever dreamed. Which was the green-eyed contessa with red hair? The emeralds for her. We could make up the hair spray, and a bracelet and a huge ring...'

They spent the rest of the morning at the shop, had lunch together, returned to the shop to continue the discussion and plans for most of the afternoon.

About four-thirty, Pietro stopped them firmly. 'We will be late for the concert, cara,' he told his wife. 'It is scheduled for five and usually is begun by five-fifteen. Come. Where is your cloak?'

'I'll take care of all this!' Andy called after them, as they left. Veronica waved back at him.

'He is very efficient,' she praised him timidly to her husband. Pietro nodded.

'Yes, he knows his business. The ladies will be pleased with their jewellery.'

126

Cool praise, but better than none. She was silent as they drove to the Pergola. She noticed now that the driver was accompanied by another man, both big and tough looking men. Pietro seemed as alert as he had been in Palermo and in Naples.

She frowned a little, puzzled. Surely danger would not touch them in Florence.

She forgot them in the excitement of the concert. The Pergola was a beautiful theatre, and they had a box near the stage. She gazed down at the quartet of musicians, dreamed over the lovely music of Beethoven as they played several of the more famous quartets. Pietro leaned over the back of her chair, and occasionally touched her hair lightly, or her bare shoulder, her arm, whispering to her between the movements.

'Look across at the box opposite, the third one. That is the English duchess I told you about. With her is the Marchese and his wife—I will introduce you at intermission—they sent us a wedding gift of a silver tea set. You recall.'

'Yes. How kind.'

'They were friends of my father. Next to them is the Ruggeri box. I used to know the family.'

His tone had hardened. He bowed his head in curt acknowledgement as someone moved a hand in that box. Veronica lifted her opera-glasses, casually, looked at the stage, then moments later looked across at the boxes opposite. A raven-haired beauty was in the box, looking her way. A beauty, yes, with creamy skin, a magnificent red silk dress embroidered in pearls...

Veronica dropped the glasses into her lap. She stared again at the stage, not seeing it, not hearing the glorious strains of the violins as they soared up and up into the quiet air of the theatre. The beauty—with a smile on her red lips and a contemptuous look...

Slowly she lifted her hand, and touched the slim dog-collar of pearls, the three strands her father had designed for her. She wore her blue silk dress, the one Pietro liked best. Her hair was dressed simply, but elegantly, and she wore a spray of diamonds and pearls in it. Did she look so dowdy? Why was the beauty looking so amused and contemptuous of her? The dress was new, in the latest style, her skirts flaring, her waist slim. But the dress was not cut low. Pietro did not like low-cut bosoms. Not in his wife. The beauty wore hers so low one did not need to guess about the shape of her firm breasts.

Veronica burned with anger? shame? jealousy? She wasn't sure.

At the intermission, Pietro took her around the boxes, introduced her, seemingly proud of her, to several friends. He did not go around to the other side. The Marchese came their way, and met them in the lobby. Veronica met their searching appraisal, smiled bravely, spoke little. She did not contradict her husband when he explained she was just learning Italian.

'What beauty,' she heard one man say. Pietro smiled. 'What a lovely blonde beauty. She is English? No? American? Beautiful. You found her in New York City? I must go to that city!' the man teased Pietro, in Italian, in a low tone.

When they returned to the box, Pietro asked her, 'Did you understand all their compliments, cara?'

'I understood some, Pietro,' she said. 'I hope...I hope I did not look...' she hesitated.

'Look how?' He laid her cloak back around the chair. 'Are you warm enough, cara? There is a draught here, I think.'

'Yes, warm enough. I meant...did I look fashionable enough?'

'You are as beautiful as a princess, cara,' he assured her, his voice caressing.

But he did not say she was fashionable, she thought, as the music began again. During the second half of the concert, she stole little glances in her opera glasses at the Italian girl in the box opposite. She was gloriously beautiful, opulent, with diamonds sparkling in her ears, at her throat. Her bodice was embroidered with pearls and diamonds. Her hair was dressed high, her tiara was large, too large, thought Veronica, critically. She was—gaudy. Too much. That decided, the girl turned back to the music. But she kept looking at Regina Ruggeri, her rival.

The woman was tall, gaudy, glowingly beautiful. The opposite of Veronica, who was blonde, small, quietly pretty. Was Regina the type that Pietro truly admired?

Her heart began to ache again, the way it had during Giorgio's dramatic recital.

Applause startled her. The quartet rose, bowed, left the stage. They returned for more bows, then the lights came on. The concert was over.

Pietro rose, helped settle her cloak about her. 'Shall we find a restaurant and dine in Florence, cara? Would that please you?'

'No, let's go home, Pietro. It isn't late. We shall be in time for dinner, shan't we?' Now she longed for the sanctuary of her home, her Villa d'Oro. She had new thoughts to think, new problems to solve, and an ache to puzzle over.

'Do you truly wish to return home? I thought

you might enjoy an evening out. There is a restaurant...' He was saying as they made their way out slowly through the thick crowd. 'We will get our carriage at the end of the street, near the cathedral. I told our men to wait there.'

'Whatever you wish, Pietro.'

'No, it is as you wish, cara. Tell me...' He was saying, as they moved slowly down the street. The crowd thinned out, the further they moved from the concert hall.

Someone brushed against Veronica. She turned to protest as the man brushed again more heavily.

She saw a knife gleam in the hand of a thick-set man. She screamed, involuntarily. People turned. Pietro moved like a flash of lightning.

He was struggling with the man, his hand gripped in the other man's free hand. Blades flashed.

'Cavalcanti!' yelled Pietro, in a strong bellow. 'Cavalcanti! To me. To me!'

Veronica shrank against the wall, and was suddenly grasped by another man. A blade flashed at her throat. She shrieked, then her voice was stifled as the man grabbed at her dog collar of pearls. A wrench, pain, she was struggling futilely in the arms of a man twice her size. Pietro was still fighting another man, on

131

the sidewalk three feet from her.

'No, no,' she cried, muffled. She tried to fight, but he was too strong. The blade flashed.

A cold stroke into her shoulder. And she knew the knife had gone in. She moaned, as the coldness turned to blinding hot pain. The pain increased as the knife was pulled out, yanked out, and the man's bright eyes blazed down at her.

'Madonna!' a man cried, and a knife slashed at her attacker. The man whirled around, ducked among the men, fled. An older man, someone she dimly recognized, caught her as she slumped against the wall. She felt his strong arms lifting her, holding her.

It was over in moments. Pietro's two men had come, had fought off one man from their master. Now Pietro dashed to her side. The Marchese was holding her in his arms.

'Pietro—she has been knifed,' he said, quietly, in Italian. 'You must allow me to help her.'

'My God...my God, madonna mia, madre di Dios...' Pietro whispered as he took Veronica from the Marchese. His hand shook as he uncovered her shoulder. The cloak was bloody, she could see, and her dress, her blue silk was torn about the wound.

'My God...' the whisper ran through the theatre crowd. As Veronica gazed up at the anxious circle of faces, she recognized them, the men and women she had met, closed protectively around her and Pietro. Several of the men held knives, shielding them only after a few minutes of waiting.

'The villains have left, Pietro. Come, we will carry her to a doctor.' The Marchese seemed to have taken charge. Pietro and two men lifted her, the carriage was brought. Then Veronica blanked out as she was put into the carriage.

She roused once as the doctor probed at her, with seeming cruelty. She cried out, again, as he cleaned the wound. Pietro's face seemed white as he held her tightly and whispered to her to be careful, to be quiet, to hold still.

The pain seemed to blaze through her whole body, burning, stinging, settling finally into a steady rough pain that hurt and hurt and hurt. Her throat ached from screaming, and from the roughness with which the thief had snatched her dog collar of pearls. The pearls—her father's design—She moaned, softly, turned her face against Pietro's chest.

'That's it. It is better if she faints,' said the Marchese, with compassion. 'Pietro, my son, bring her to my home. We will care for her as for our own. Come, it is late and dark. They might return.'

'Thank you, but I will return home, we will

take her home,' said Pietro. 'If you will loan me four men...'

'But naturally. And I too will come with you,' he said, with decision. 'Is she ready, doctor?'

'I have done all possible,' said the rough voice, in hearty Tuscan dialect. 'Now she must rest and sleep. Better if she is home.'

During the long ride up the hill. Veronica was only half-conscious. But she was aware of how her husband held her closely, how he whispered to her, whispered prayers, anxiously. And in spite of the horror she had gone through, she felt safe in his arms.

CHAPTER 8

It was more than a week before Veronica could sit up, free of fever, and beginning to feel like herself again. The arm still pained her intensely, from shoulder to wrist, but the wound in the shoulder had begun to heal and itch.

Pietro crept quietly into her room that morning, smiled radiantly to see her awake, and laid a yellow rose on her pillow.

'Cara, you feel better today?' he murmured.

She nodded, her blonde hair stirring on the pillow as she moved her head. 'Much better, I slept well. Pietro, are you still staying up?' she added reproachfully, as she noted the intense dark shadows under his eyes.

'How can I sleep when you are so ill?' he asked simply. He sat down beside the bed, gazed at her tenderly. 'I think you are truly better, cara. Your eyes are brighter, your face has good colour. Does the shoulder feel better now?'

She moved her arm slowly, carefully, then nodded in relief. 'Much much better, Pietro. It itches, it doesn't pain so much. And you must sleep!'

'Later,' he said. He touched her cheek gently, brushed his fingers over her forehead. 'The fever is gone, your face is cool now. Thank God!'

She shivered a little as memory of the attack returned. A shadow crossed her face. 'Pietro, have you discovered who...' she began.

'Hush, cara, leave the matter to me,' he said, frowning. 'I have posted guards. I do not wish you worried about anything. I will take care of the matter!'

He was his old dictatorial self, she thought with amusement, and reached out slowly to take his hand. He closed his fingers around her hand, and they sat in contented silence for a while until the old maid Maddalena brought her morning coffee and rolls.

The doctor came again that day, and pronounced himself satisfied with the way the wound was healing. He told her she might lie on the balcony for a while in the sunshine, it would do her good.

Two of the servants set up a lounge on the balcony outside her bedroom, and Pietro carried her out tenderly, and set her on the lounge. They propped her up with pillows, and Camilla tucked blankets around her.

'Oh, the sunlight, so delicious,' said Veronica, closing her eyes happily, lifting her face to the light. Pietro sat with her for a long time, later Camilla came and sat with her while Pietro worked in his study.

'You don't need to guard me,' Veronica finally protested to Camilla. 'Truly you don't. You must have so much else to do—the housework, the meal planning—'

'That is all finished for today,' said Camilla, stitching away on a little piece of silk. 'I am happy to be with you. Later we will have lessons in Italian and English.'

Camilla did not say that they were guarding her, but Veronica noticed the following week that either Camilla or Pietro would remain with her constantly. Were they troubled about the knife wound, or did they fear another attack? There were shadows under Camilla's eyes, and her gentle face seemed older and more worried.

The whole household rejoiced when she came down for her first meal. They hovered around beaming, and even the outdoor servants peeped through the kitchen door at her. 'Now, the house is well again,' said Maddalena, and the cook prepared a special elaborate torta for dessert.

Even Giorgio and Uncle Teodosio were aroused to unusual expressions of pleasure. Veronica was touched when Pietro's uncle lifted her hand to his lips, and proclaimed sonorously, 'The sunlight has returned! We thank God and the Blessed Virgin!'

Veronica thought she had never seen Pietro look so happy and pleased. Camilla kept smiling and smiling, her eyes sometimes wet with tears through the meal and the evening in the yellow salon. Friends had sent flowers all through her convalescence, baskets of flowers, vases, bouquets filled the hallway, the yellow salon, the library, and her bedroom upstairs.

A huge basket of mums caught Veronica's attention. They stood in the corner of the yellow salon, yellow mums, and pale fuchsia ones. She exclaimed over them, and asked who had sent them.

Camilla looked uneasy. 'It was a friend of yours, Veronica, a lady named Miss Diana Jansson. She sent a note that she wished to visit with you whenever you were recovered enough.'

'Diana! Oh, that is wonderful! She must have hastened through her trip to Naples and Rome. Pietro, isn't that fine? When can we have her?'

'Whenever you wish, cara,' said Pietro, leaning back, and relaxing in the cushions of the couch beside her. He patted her hand. 'Whenever you wish something, you have but to ask.'

'Bad taste,' said Giorgio bluntly in Italian, looking at the mums.

Veronica looked at him, rather startled. Was he criticizing Pietro's display of affection?

'Giorgio, do not say that,' said Camilla, blushing. 'She is an American, she didn't know. It is the flowers, Veronica. We do not usually send the chrysanthemums to friends. It is considered...ah...bad luck. Sometimes.'

'It is the flower we use to send to the dead,' said Giorgio, calmly. 'They are called the flowers of the dead. They are sent to funerals. Also they are on our Memorial Day, you see.'

'Giorgio!' said Pietro sharply, his face stern. 'You are not to say that...'

Giorgio shrugged. 'It is the truth,' he said.

'But as Camilla has remarked, the American lady did not know this custom. Of course, it means nothing. The flowers are pretty.'

Veronica turned away from the sight of the gay basket. She felt uneasy, depressed as though a brush of grey evil had whispered past her face. But of course Diana could not have known about the custom, she had just arrived in Italy. Still that sinister encounter on the streets near the Pergola, the knife stabbing, the attempt on her life, added to her father's death from arsenic poisoning... She stared down at her thin hands, twisting together on her lap. Camilla had helped her put on a new blue velvet dress, one that Pietro had ordered for her. She smoothed the velvet fondly, thinking about Pietro, forcing herself to think only of Pietro and his care of her. He would protect her, he would not let anything terrible happen to her.

Camilla was studying her face anxiously. She jumped up. 'You have not seen the violets of the Marchese,' she said, and brought over a beautiful rare vase of pink filled with exquisite deep purple violets. 'They are from his greenhouses. Are they not lovely?'

Veronica took the vase in her hands. 'Oh, lovely, yes, and how delicious the scent.' She took a deep breath of the beautiful flowers, and smiled with delight at them.

Pietro shifted his legs uneasily. 'They are like the ones which—ah—Andy Kelly brought to you. Pink roses of the month and purple Parma violets. I believe you might have been too feverish to remember them.'

Veronica thought of the small basket she vaguely remembered in her feverish dreams, the scent that had been touching and sweet. 'Yes, I do remember. How kind of Andy.'

'I kept the basket for you,' said Camilla, and blushed unexpectedly. 'I thought you might wish to keep it.'

Pietro cleared his throat. 'He has been kind,' said her husband stiffly, unwillingly. 'He has written several notes. I will show them to you when you wish.'

She knew what an effort it was for her husband to make that concession. 'Thank you, Pietro,' she said quietly. 'Later we will talk about the business. Just tell me now, have the jewellery orders been well begun for the Rome ladies?'

He nodded, relaxing. 'Yes, Andy made up the emeralds at once, they were taken to Rome, and were highly approved. I have heard that the contessa, the red-haired one, you recall her, was so pleased that she is announcing everywhere how good our jewellery is. We have several more orders from Rome, and have hired two more men in the shop.'

'Oh, that's good, that's wonderful,' sighed Veronica, happy to have some pleasant news.

That night, she was awake when her husband crept into her room, bent over her, listened to her breathing anxiously.

She stirred, and lifted her good right hand sleepily to touch his face. 'I am awake, Pietro. I am all right, darling.'

'Did I waken you? I am sorry. I was anxious...'

'No, no, I was just awake. Darling, please get some sleep. I am truly all right.'

Instead he sat down on the bed, and caressed her hand. 'If you knew how I felt,' he whispered. 'Those nights of agony, those days of wondering what I could have done to prevent this terrible thing...'

'You did all you could and more, darling.' She turned slowly on her side, her shoulder throbbing painfully as she moved. 'And you stopped them. And the Marchese and his men—how grandly they came—you have good friends here, Pietro. When you called, they came at once.'

'As in the old days,' he said, musingly. 'Our ancestors fought on the same side through centuries of troubles in Florence. Little did I think to utter that battle cry again to warn of danger.' She saw his head moving, darkly in the shadowy room. Moonlight flowed across her bed, sometimes touching his face, sometimes glinting from his dark hair. 'But I must let you sleep, darling. Sometime, I will tell you of the old days, and the history of my family, which shall be the family of our children.'

She felt a thrill as he spoke of this simply, touched her hand, kissed her forehead tenderly, and left her. The door stayed opened between their rooms, and she knew that a word from her would bring him at once to help her.

A few days later, days spent lying on the balcony in the sunshine, wrapped in blankets, Diana Jansson and her aunt came to visit them. The aunt was left in the yellow salon with poor Camilla to entertain the deaf woman. Diana was shown up to Veronica's balcony.

The taller girl swept in grandly from the living room of Veronica's suite, over to the place where she lay propped up on cushions. She wore a travelling cloak of silver-grey, and a stunning dress of blue and silver velvet. Her greenish-grey eyes were deeply concerned as she bent to kiss Veronica's cheek.

'Darling, how worried I am. How are you, my dearest?'

'I'm healing well, Diana. Do sit down. How

kind you were to send the gorgeous flowers!'
Again she thought of the mums, their meaning revealed so carelessly by Giorgio. Flowers
of the dead! She shivered in the bright sunlight,
and turned on her smile another brighter glow..
'And all your notes. Pietro brought them to
me.'

'All Florence is talking about the tragedy,'
said Diana, perching on the edge of the chair,
and surveying her keenly. 'What did happen,
Veronica? Are you too weary to talk?'

Oddly enough, Veronica did feel weary. The
wound was healing nicely, but she had little
strength. She felt apathetic, as though her
eyelids would not stay open. Perhaps it was the
bright sunshine, she thought.

'I don't feel very stong, Diana. Please, let us
just talk. Tell me about Naples and Rome. Did
you enjoy your trip?'

Diana settled back, and chatted very sweetly about her travels. She described Rome in
glowing terms. 'Darling, we stayed there more
than two weeks. I sketched, walked about, sat
in outdoor cafes, and sketched more and more.
I have ideas for some paintings I want to do.
Poor auntie, she was quite exhausted with all
the walking, and assented very eagerly when
I asked to come on to Florence. You know,
darling, I must have sensed something was

wrong. No sooner had I arrived, than I heard about the dreadful attack on the Cavalcantis. My dearest friend, attacked on the streets of this beautiful city! My heart almost failed me.'

The talk kept returning again and again to the attack. Veronica felt quite weary with it all. Yet Diana was so sweet and concerned, she could not insult her by abruptly sending her away. She told about the attack, Diana listened as though to a medieval fairy tale.

'And the Marchese himself came to your help? How gallant, how chivalrous! And the men all carry knives? How primitive, my darling girl! Where have you arrived? What kind of country is this? It seemed so civilized, yet these attacks on you...'

Underneath the sweetness, Veronica sensed a contempt for her adopted country. She protested vigorously, sitting up straight on the cushions.

'The Italians are wonderful people! Of course, they are civilized. Italy—Rome and Florence—were settled and cultured places a thousand years before America was discovered! Don't pretend that New York City is not a dangerous place! One can't go out without a guard at night!'

'Darling, darling, how fierce you are!' Diana began laughing. She patted Veronica soothingly on her hand. Veronica flinched, it was her wounded arm. Diana did not seem to notice. 'Of course they are civilized! I just can't help worrying, though...' And her greenish-grey eyes turned troubled again. 'Your father—he did die suddenly, didn't he?'

'No, he was ill almost a year,' said Veronica, lying back on the cushions again. She watched Diana's sweet face, the lights flickering across the lovely creamy cheeks and forehead, the expressions of her red mouth. She wished she could confide in Diana, she would understand. But some caution kept her quiet.

Diana was shaking her head slowly. 'It seems so strange, that you should be attacked. What could be the motive?'

'The men stole a valuable strand of pearls,' said Veronica bluntly. 'Here—you can see the marks yet on my throat where the man yanked the dog collar of pearls from me. I imagine that would sell well.'

'Then robbery was the motive?' asked Diana, frowning a little. 'Yes, it could be. For they attacked *you*, not Pietro, at first, didn't they?'

Diana kept on and on. Veronica huddled in the cushions, wishing she would go back to Florence. She felt feverish and light-headed, weary, so very tired.

145

Finally Pietro appeared in the doorway to Veronica's bedroom. He looked surprised to see Diana Jansson there, but came forward courteously.

'Miss Jansson, I am so sorry. They did not inform me you were here!' He looked searchingly at Veronica. His wife could not even summon a smile.

Diana had jumped up girlishly, flirtatious automatically in the presence of a handsome man. 'Oh, Pietro—may I call you Pietro? I have been having such a good talk with Veronica! This terrible attack—my poor little child! She is so small, so frail...'

'Yes, and I am afraid she is weary,' said Pietro, more bluntly than usual. 'Let us go downstairs and allow me to show you the gardens. They are especially lovely in the fall. Veronica, I will send Maddalena. You should return to bed, cara. You are looking very weary.'

He brusquely took Diana away, and must have turned her over to Camilla, for he returned in time to help Maddalena settle her in her wide comfortable bed, in the shadowy bedroom. Veronica settled in the bed with a great sigh of relief.

'That woman...' he fumed, as he helped Veronica get settled. 'Another cushion under your head, cara? No? That Miss Jansson, she has worn you out. She did not even write she was coming. If I had known, I would have let her stay only a little short time.'

Veronica managed a smile, but it must have been a tired one. He shooed Maddalena away, closed the drapes, and told Veronica to sleep. She was not called for dinner. Pietro and Camilla brought up a small tray later at night when she was awake again.

Veronica listened to Camilla and Pietro with some amusement as they quarrelled over her.

'But Pietro, she is a friend of Veronica. I thought she would wish to visit without interruption!' wailed Camilla.

'No friend is a friend who visits so long with a sick woman,' said Pietro. 'Come, cara, a little more broth.'

'And that deaf aunt, so terrible to talk to,' Camilla sniffed. Their Italian rattled along so rapidly that Veronica could scarcely follow. 'All I understood was that they had been rushed through Naples and Rome and up to Florence before she had a chance to see Rome.'

Veronica frowned a little. Had she understood Camilla correctly? Or had Camilla misunderstood the aunt? 'They had a week in Naples and two weeks in Rome,' she said weakly.

Camilla would have argued the point, but Pietro ordered her away autocratically, and sat beside Veronica until she fell asleep again.

Veronica felt too weak to get up the next day. Pietro went around with a worried scowl, and made Camilla cry by telling her it was her fault.

Veronica tried to smooth things over, but Camilla was very subdued and unhappy for several days.

Finally Veronica was able to get up again. Pietro said, 'No visitors,' and posted Giorgio as guard when he himself had to go down to Florence on business. Veronica lay on the lounge, soaking up the early November sunlight, gazing down at the flower beds, where a gardener worked vigorously over the roses and green bushes.

It seemed so strange for it to be November. In New York, she thought, the rains would have started, and perhaps an early snowfall would have made black slush on the city streets. Here the sky was a brilliant blue, the clouds were sparce and gloriously puffy white like so many white flowers spilled in a blue bowl.

She lay by the hour, watching the clouds moved along languidly by a light breeze. Toward evening, as the sun began spilling colours across the sky, banners of pink and rose and orange, she began to hear the bells from Florence, tinkling, and ringing, and making their joyous holy music in the sunset.

Evening shadows spilled lightly across the wide green lawns, the white gravelled path along one side, on the yellow roses and the red roses, and the green bushes, trimmed in stern order. The fountain splashed lightly, making a bubbling sound, and she could see the white dolphin as it blew water into the air. It was so peaceful, so beautiful, her home, her Villa d'Oro.

Her heart grew lighter. Nothing terrible could happen to her in this beautiful home, the home of her husband, Pietro. Her beloved husband—

She loved him, she thought, suddenly. Wide-eyed she gazed down at the green lawns, up at the sky which was turning from rose to blue to purple of night. She loved Pietro. How long had she loved him? She didn't know. She just knew now that she did love him. How slowly and secretly had love come to her!

Bells were ringing in her heart, even as the bells of Florence were ringing in the valley, a soft singing musical happiness. She loved him. He was so tender, so gentle, yet so strong, so possessive and determined to protect her. He had made love to her so carefully at first, then

149

that one night, with such intense passion that it had overwhelmed her.

She wished—how she wished, that she were well again, and he could feel free to come to her bed and make love to her again!

A yellow rose dropped in her lap!

She started, and turned up her rosy happy face to Pietro, who was bending over her with a smile.

'Were you asleep, cara?' he asked, the caress strong in his tone.

'No, no, just dreaming, wide awake,' she confessed. 'I was looking at the lovely lawns, at the sky, hearing the bells, it is so beautiful here, so lovely in my new home...'

He bent and kissed her cheek, then pressed his face against hers. 'You are happy here, in spite of the terrible thing that happened?' he asked, anxiously.

'So happy, so very happy,' she assured him.

He sat down beside her, and she lifted the yellow rose and smelled it deeply. He had removed the thorns one by one, as he always did before he brought the rose to her.

'I am happy also, cara,' he told her, simply. 'Beyond my biggest dreams, I am happy. If only you were well, I should be so happy, I would be able to float in the air.'

She lifted her face from the rose, and looked

deeply into his dark eyes. 'Oh, Pietro...I'm glad...' She whispered the words, lifted her one hand timidly toward him. He bent again, kissed her mouth gently, as though afraid to hurt her. 'I am better, much better,' she assured him, then blushed. Would he think it was a bold invitation.

'I had thought to tell you about the past, cara,' he said, sitting back, his dark head against the cushions of the comfortable chair. 'But I find myself thinking more and more eagerly about the future. You know, the business is going better than I had imagined. Your father had such plans for it, and we—you and I and Andy Kelly and the others—I think we shall be able to carry out his dreams for him. Surely, he knows this. Perhaps he knew this when he approved of our marriage. Perhaps he sensed that we would be able to carry out his dreams.'

'Oh, Pietro, I hope he does know it.' Her hand reached out again, and he clasped it in his. In the darkening evening, he talked to her eagerly about the plans. What her father had said to him, how he had planned to expand the business in Italy, how he wanted to turn to the more expensive gems, to design more beautiful jewellery in New York and in Florence.

Then Pietro began to talk more intimately

about themselves. She listened with quickening heart as he spoke.

'I hope so much for a child, cara,' he told her, with his almost terrifying frankness. 'I want a son, several sons if God wills it. And daughters too. I am a very demanding man, cara! At first, I thought perhaps you were too involved with the business, that you might not care for this. But lately, I think perhaps you feel as I do—that you will perhaps learn to love me, and to wish for my children, for our children...'

In the growing darkness, he seemed able to talk more frankly than ever. She pressed his hand with her fingers, strongly, feeling the tension in his. 'I do...wish for a child, for several, Pietro,' she whispered. 'I too wish for children. It would make me so very happy. A baby... perhaps within a year, if God wills.'

He leaned closer to her, and pressed his cheek against hers. Always so tender, so gentle—her heart seemed to swell within her chest until it was almost painful. Oh, how she wished she was not just recovering from the wound!

He might then have picked her up and taken her inside, to his bedroom, to his bed.

But they stayed on the balcony and talked for a long time, of the future, of their plans, their hopes. Maybe it was a good thing the attack had happened, she thought. If it had not, if she had rushed around, working at the shop, seeing Andy of whom Pietro was jealous, Pietro might not have confided in her so soon. He might not have come to love and trust her, to feel protectively toward her. Her very illness might have brought them closer together.

CHAPTER 9

Veronica grew more and more puzzled at her own weakness. The wound had healed, leaving an ugly scar in her shoulder. The doctor assured her it had healed well, that the scar would fade in time from the dark red to pink then to a white gash.

Still she felt languid and weak. Camilla sat with her every morning, sewing and chatting, while Pietro did his work in his study, or went down to Florence to check on orders. He did not attempt a trip to Rome, and Veronica knew he was deeply concerned about her lack of progress.

Camilla came in early one morning, before Maddalena had brought Veronica's coffee. She

153

sat down beside the bed, and looked gravely at her sister-in-law.

'Veronica, my dear sister,' she said, very gently. 'Do you trust me at all?'

'Trust you?' Veronica gasped. 'But of course! You are my dearest friend!' She touched Camilla's hand.

Camilla clasped the hand with her warm ones. 'My darling, trust me very much today. I have brought a jar with a lid. After Maddalena brings your coffee, I want you to pretend to sip it, then send the maid away. Then I will pour your coffee into the jar and take it to Florence when I go shopping there today.'

Veronica felt herself growing colder and colder there in her warm bed. She stared up at Camilla. Her face must have gone white. Camilla bent over her, murmuring her alarm.

'Darling don't be upset! Oh, Pietro will be so angry if I upset you!'

'What do you think? What do you suspect?' Veronica managed to gasp.

'I don't know. I cannot believe this,' said Camilla simply. 'But...I talked one day to Andy Kelly.' Her face began to redden like a little rose, but she kept on bravely. 'I liked him, trusted him. He confided in me about your father's death. From poisoning. Oh, cara, I must find out! I am beginning to believe... You

154

see, I have traded cups with you at the table, traded wine glasses, traded food plates. You did not suspect?'

She smiled proudly.

'No, I never guessed. Does Pietro...'

'He does not know yet. He will blow up like a volcano, I promise you, if this is true! But I must find out.'

She stopped abruptly. Maddalena had tapped at the door, and now slid in on her slippered feet, her innocent old face rimmed with white stringy hair, her eyes anxious. 'Do you wake up now?' she asked in Italian. 'I bring you coffee, signora.'

Camilla stood up, and went over to the window. 'It looks like a lovely day for my trip to Florence.' she said, in Italian.

Maddalena set the tray down on the bedside table. Her face beamed as Veronica sat up slowly. She bent over the girl, plumped up the pillows vigorously, helped her lean against them.

'Better today, yes, yes?' she asked hopefully. 'Does the lady feel much better today?'

Veronica gazed into her innocent face, at the dark eyes, snapping and sparkling. She could not believe the maid would poison her. What had gotten into Camilla's brain?

'I feel better, thank you,' she said, in Italian.

'Thank you, Maddalena, that will be all for now. Please bring my breakfast in an hour.'

'Yes, yes, signora, I will do it all,' said the maid happily. She set the small silver tray on Veronica's lap, hovered over her.

Veronica took one sip. The coffee was hot, milky, strong. Was there a bitter taste? Italian coffee had always tasted more bitter to her than American.

The maid left, and closed the door after her. Camilla returned from the window, and stood over Veronica. Silently, Veronica handed her the coffee cup. Camilla produced a glass bottle from her pocket, and poured the coffee into it.

'And I will pour out the rest of the coffee from the pitcher also,' she said, firmly, and went to the balcony, and threw it out among the roses. 'There,' she said, returning, her eyes sparkling. 'Today, I shall find out! You see, your breakfast coffee is the only thing I have not traded with you. And I feel no effects, no weakness.'

'But my father... He was poisoned in New York, Camilla! I always thought Dr Heinrich...and he is not here...'

'I must find out,' she said, more firmly and decisively than Veronica had thought she was capable of being. Camilla was growing up,

156

maturing. 'Something is happening to you, and it is not the wound. Well, I shall go first to a chemist, I have a friend and her brother is a chemist, and he will be honest with me. And he will do the analysis quickly, and so I will know when I return today.'

Veronica chewed thoughtfully on the small roll. It felt dry without her usual hot coffee. How much she had depended on her coffee, she thought. She had drunk it eagerly each morning, feeling the warmth and stimulation pouring through her. But by afternoon, she was again languid, weak, caring nothing for anything.

'If this is true...' she said, in a low tone. 'What can I believe? Who poisoned my father?'

'One matter at a time, that is what Pietro says,' said the young girl firmly. She bent and kissed Veronica's cheek warmly. 'Dearest Veronica, take care of yourself today. It is cool on the balcony, remember it is mid-November, and keep a blanket on yourself, and call Pietro to bring you in if it is chilly.'

Pietro strolled in unexpectedly from his bedroom. 'What is all this? You are ordering my wife about?' he asked, a merry twinkle in his eyes. 'Do you think she is incapable of managing without you for a day, little sister?'

Veronica noticed that Camilla had hidden the

157

bottle of coffee behind her as soon as she heard the door opening. Why did Camilla conceal anything from Pietro? Shrewdly she guessed that it was because her information about poisoning had come from Andy Kelly, of whom Pietro was jealous. But, was there a deeper reason? Did Camilla not trust her own brother?

Veronica felt a new chill as she considered that thought. Pietro and Camilla were chatting about her errands. Did Camilla not really trust her older brother? What hidden depths were in the girl. Did she have a reason not to trust Pietro?

'Oh, dear God, dear blessed Virgin Mary,' thought Veronica, in a cold panic. If she couldn't trust Pietro, whom could she trust? To whom could she turn? Pietro had been in New York during the time of her father's poisoning! Maybe it had not been Sybil's doctor at all, not her stepmother, and the man who wanted her.

Perhaps it had been Pietro!

Poisoning.

She remembered the stories of the Medici family, of the intrigues in Italy, of the poisonings, the strange happenings to Italian families.

She gazed up at her husband's strong face. His mouth was twisted in irony at something his sister was saying. He looked cool, hard, strong, as though capable of anything. His dark eyes, so shuttered and unfathomable at times.

She remembered what Giorgio had confided to her, of Pietro's love for the Italian beauty. Of his anger at her, his coldness and hardness after he discovered her marriage, her willingness to take him as a lover.

She thought, 'Yes, he can be hard and calculating. I think so. But would he—poison? Would he? Oh, God, I don't know! I have to trust him blindly... But does Camilla trust him? Even his own sister?'

Camilla had turned to her, she had hidden the bottle in her pocket deftly when her brother was turned from her gaze. 'Veronica, darling, shall I bring you anything from Florence? Flowers, sweets? Anything at all?'

Veronica shook her head weakly. 'Nothing, darling. Just be careful.'

'They won't dare touch Camilla,' said Pietro, suddenly angry. 'If they did—I shall kill with my bare hands!'

He looked devilish for a moment. Veronica shivered again. He softened, bent over her, pulled up the blanket.

'Don't worry, cara, I am sending two men besides the driver and her chaperon. Also, the Marchese is watching over ours. His men are everywhere, he told me. She will be guarded every minute of the time.'

Camilla looked rather nervous at this. Pietro went out with Camilla, and Veronica heard them talking as they went down the stairs to breakfast.

Later Maddalena brought her breakfast. Veronica picked over it listlessly. She didn't feel hungry when she thought there might be poison in the food. Maddalena clucked over the tray as she took it away.

Pietro came up. 'It is rather cool on the balcony, darling, but the fresh air does you good. Shall I help you out there? Camilla will be leaving soon, you can wave to her!'

'I wish...I wish I could go with her,' she said suddenly, as Pietro helped her out of bed. 'Well, someday soon I'll be strong enough, really.'

'Of course you will,' he said, heartily. But he still looked worried. 'Today we shall have lunch together on the balcony. That will be pleasant. Soon enough, there will be much colder weather, perhaps some snow, and we shall have to keep you indoors.'

Pietro stayed with her half the morning, talking, or sitting on the chair near her looking out at the lawns where the gardener clipped industriously at the neat hedges. 'He never does what I tell him,' said Pietro, exasperated.

'Today I told him to work on potting the flowers to put in the shed for the winter. I shall go down and speak to him again.'

Pietro disappeared, reappeared a few minutes later in the gardens. The man listened to him, his head bent. Finally he went away with Pietro.

Veronica lay on her lounge chair, warmly covered with blankets, and thought about Camilla. The girl was wandering freely about in Florence, vigorous and young and strong. In and out of the lovely shops, followed by her patient chaperon, the maid Maria. She could see the gorgeous silks, the leather shops, sit in a coffee shop and have her lunch in an elegant restaurant.

She might see Andy Kelly at the Murray shop, and talk to him. And this afternoon—before she left—she would return to the store of her friend, the chemist, and pick up the analysis of Veronica's coffee.

Veronica shuddered in the strong sunlight, and huddled under the blanket. Poison. It was such a chilling, unpleasant thought. Like the cold knife sliding into her shoulder, to emerge blazing with pain.

The hours dragged. She refused coffee with her lunch, picked at her food until Pietro was very concerned. 'At least, have some fruit, cara.

You will waste away! Where is your appetite?'

She had looked at the food, thought poison, and lost all her desire for food. Yet she was hungry. 'Fruit, I will have some fruit,' she said, impulsively. No one could poison an orange, could they?

Pietro's worried face lightened, and he peeled the small sweet orange for her carefully. When she ate it hungrily, he promptly prepared another one for her, and watched in satisfaction as she ate that one also.

'Perhaps you do not care for Italian cooking, cara,' he said anxiously. 'The pasta all the time. Do you prefer meats, vegetables? I shall have them prepare more salads for you. Tell me what you wish, and they shall prepare it at once.'

'No, no, Pietro. This is fine,' she said hastily, visualizing poison in her green salads. 'Usually I like spaghetti—and I love it with clam sauce. And the green noodles—those are so good.'

'You shall have the spaghetti with clam sauce tomorrow, and the green noodles the next day,' he said, at once. 'I shall give orders!'

She looked at him with some amusement and exasperation. He was so persistent and so bossy! But he was concerned about her, and that concern made her feel better.

Maybe Camilla's guess was wrong. It might be that wound had caused some trouble in her body, and that was what kept her so languid and weak.

She waited more and more impatiently for Camilla's return from Florence. She refused to be moved indoors at dusk, to Pietro's concern. 'I want to see Camilla drive up,' she said.

'But cara, it is cold out here! And she will return on time, I promise you! I will send her upstairs to you at once, will that please you?' He studied her face anxiously.

'No, please, I want to wait out here.' She pressed his hand weakly. 'Please, Pietro. Please.'

She sighed as he finally agreed. He waited there with her until they saw the carriage rolling in the long driveway, up toward the house.

'Now, will you go inside, or must you wait?'

'I will wait. Go down and greet her, please. I will wait up here on the balcony,' she said.

He shook his head at her obstinacy. But he left her to go down and greet his sister. He helped Camilla out of the carriage. Veronica leaned forward intently, looking down. Pietro said something to his sister. Camilla gazed up and waved at her. She did not smile. Her face was fiercely intent.

163

Veronica felt a fresh wave of despair. She fell back on the lounge chair and waited. But she knew.

Soon Camilla had run up the stairs, and through the drawing room of Veronica's suite, out to the balcony and along it to Veronica's lounge. She fell on her knees and burst into tears. Veronica touched the dark hair tenderly.

'It is true?' Veronica asked, in Italian. In Camilla's state, she might not be able to understand English. She was too agitated.

'Si, si, si. Oh, the horror of it,' Camilla cried out. 'Oh, I will kill somebody, I will die myself—oh, the horror—'

Pietro had followed his sister, in time to hear her words. He reached them, gazed down at them thoughtfully.

He carried some flowers, more purple violets, more pink roses, a handful of hyacinths as darkly purple as the violets. A box of candy. He laid them on a free chair and knelt beside his sister.

'Camilla, calm yourself. Calm. What is it? What happened in Florence? You were attacked?'

She shook her head, but seemed half-hysterical, her dark eyes large and strange, her face wet with tears. She half-lifted her face, then bent down again, weeping.

164

'Do you have the report?' asked Veronica wearily. Camilla reached in her small purse and pulled out a sheet of paper. Pietro took it as Veronica would have reached for it.

'What is this?' he asked, glancing at the paper. He frowned, his face darkening. She could scarcely see him now in the dusk. 'What is it? I cannot read—yes, arsenic—arsenic? What is this? Camilla, where did you get this paper?'

She sat up, sniffing back more tears. 'From the chemist—Giovanna's brother, you know. Paolo, the chemist. He analysed Veronica's morning coffee which I brought to him. Oh, Pietro, our dear sister is being poisoned!'

Tears were rolling down Veronica's face. She was weeping along with Camilla. Camilla's storm of tears finally spent themselves. Pietro was standing beside them, ominously silent, his face dark and strange. He kept staring at the paper, but he didn't seem to read it.

Veronica shuddered convulsively. Camilla sat up.

'Oh, you are cold, dearest. We must take you inside, and plan what to do. Pietro, please help me!'

Her appeal finally aroused her brother from his hard intensity. 'Of course,' he said, very softly. He lifted Veronica up from the couch and carried her inside. He laid her on the bed, and went to light the candles beside her bed.

As the lights flared up, she saw his face, and almost screamed. He was hard, cold, his eyes flaring with such fury that he frightened her. His voice was still soft, very quiet.

'Who brings your morning coffee, Veronica? Is it Maddalena?'

She nodded. 'Always. She brings it in the morning.'

'She shall be punished. She shall be banished from here,' he said.

Camilla gasped, her eyes huge. The rims were red from her weeping. 'But Maddalena—she has been with us always! Her whole fifty years—'

'She is poisoning my wife. She shall go, and she shall be grateful if I do not kill her.' He said it so quietly that it took a minute for Veronica to absorb his words and their meaning.

'But M-Maddalena—s-she has been with you—it couldn't be her fault,' said Veronica, stammering in her confusion. She tried hard to clear her head. Camilla was deeply shocked, Pietro was about to blow up like a volcano, as Camilla had predicted. She had to be sensible. 'It must be someone else is putting the arsenic...It is like my father's death...'

'Your father?' he asked sharply, lifting his lean hard dark head. He stared down at her. 'Tell me more about this. What about your father? How did he die?'

Briefly, baldly, she explained. 'He died slowly, over a long period of months. I knew something was wrong, but the doctor—Sybil's doctor —could find nothing. He lost his strength, all his energy, he wasted away. As-as I am doing...' she ended in a whisper of fear.

'Poisoned? Arsenic? By whom?' he said, crisply.

'I don't know. But Andy Kelly and a man who was studying medicine—they dug up the body. I'm sorry I didn't tell you, Pietro. They dug it up, and found...found my father had died of arsenic poisoning. The body...was full of arsenic!' She choked over the words.

He glanced at Camilla. 'You knew this?'

Veronica was about to lie, and say she had told the girl. Camilla interrupted her. 'Andy Kelly told me this,' she said. 'He wanted help in protecting Veronica. He thought the step-mother's doctor might try again. He craves the stepmother and her money, we believe.'

'But how could—anyone—reach across the ocean—and persuade anyone to poison me?' asked Veronica.

Then her husband did blow up. The volcano

167

burst, from too long waiting. Pietro yelled and cursed as Veronica had never heard him. The two girls, wide-eyed, heard words they had never heard in all their sheltered lives.

'Mother of God. The blood of heaven—I will have someone's life for this—poison—Mary, listen to me, I will curse the house of that doctor—I will curse—by the son of God and his blood—' He was yelling in Italian.

The Italian softened the impact for Veronica. Camilla was flinching and wincing at the powerful curses, her shoulders drawing up as though to protect herself from the waves of fury. Veronica gazed up at him, wide-eyed, blinking, as the volcano blew its top and hot lava went streaming out in every direction, accompanied by steam and smoke.

It brought Giorgio and Uncle Teodosio, who had to hear the story completely from the beginning. They added their curses, their imprecations, their threats of what they would do. The three Italian men worked themselves up to such a fury that Veronica was fully convinced that half of Italy would suffer in a blood bath.

The men ran downstairs. Maddalena was fired in a dramatic outburst, with chorus, curses, wailing, and weeping and yelling, such as Veronica had never heard in her life.

'But it couldn't be Maddalena,' she protested, when Pietro finally returned, his voice hoarse.

'She was the instrument of the devil,' he told her, inflexibly. 'She has gone, with my curses following her. And anyone in this household who tries to hurt one hair of your head shall know more than my wrath! He shall know the cut of my knife in his throat!'

The volcano was cooling off, but it had left cold steel there instead. She shivered again, and wearily cuddled down in the blankets. Camilla had gone off weeping to her room. Dinner was two hours late, and no one seemed to care.

Pietro ordered thrown out all the food that Maddalena might have touched. A quivering man-servant prepared more food, and Camilla's own maid, Maria, served them at the dining room table. Veronica did not go down. Pietro himself brought dishes for her, and coaxed her into eating some.

'I watched every moment, myself, cara, eat something. No poison can be in this,' he urged. 'Mother of God, I will kill when I find out who bribed Maddalena to do this. Eat, cara, please, darling. Blood of the son of God, I will have someone's life! Lovely one, please eat a little of this pasta, it is your favourite green noodles, darling. I want to kill!'

She wanted to laugh a little, it was almost

169

humorous, the mingling of his angry fury and his anxious concern for her. His voice was musical, more than usual, like an opera singer, she thought. The aria went up and down, coaxing, pleading, imprecations following caressing words.

She managed to eat enough to please him. She could hear the servants downstairs, talking, wailing, their voices rising.

'What is going on down there? What are they saying?' she asked anxiously, fearful of more trouble.

'Giorgio and Uncle Teodosio are questioning them,' he said grimly. 'We want to learn if any more were implicated. Maddalena had second cousins here. Also she has a father who was once our butler. He shall be questioned, to see if he was approached by anyone with bribes.'

'But, Pietro,' she sighed, wearily. 'No, no more fruit. Pietro, I don't think that Maddalena knew...'

'She must have known,' he said, coldly. 'Leave this to me, cara. I wish you had told me before,' he added, reproachfully. 'You told Andy Kelly, but not your Pietro.'

She flinched. How to explain this? 'Please, Pietro, it was long ago, in New York. He offered to find out how my father had died,' she

170

said, weakly. 'I had known him a long time...'

'Longer than you had known me,' he said, simply, but with hurt in his tone. 'You could not confide in me...'

She pushed the plates away, caught at both his hands with her small ones. 'Pietro, listen to me,' she said earnestly. 'You offered me marriage, and it was sanctuary to me. I thought when I left New York I would leave danger behind. Sybil's doctor was the one I suspected. Then Andy offered to have his medical friend learn the cause. I did not want to tell you about this, and involve you without any proof. Then on the ship and again here in Florence, I was attacked, I didn't know what to think...'

'You thought I might have encouraged the attacks?' he asked, his hands stiff in hers.

'No, no, no! Never!' she told him passionately. The Italian drama had begun to affect her, she thought. She felt like singing a grand aria about her belief in him! But it was beyond her ability and her strength to say much more. 'Please, believe me, Pietro. I wanted to start again, away from Sybil. I hoped the ugliness was all over. My father...' She began to weep again, and that was all he needed. 'My father ...dying...I was so sure the doctor had killed him. Oh, Pietro, I wanted to forget...'

He gathered her in his arms and kissed her

gently, soothingly. 'Do not cry again, cara, you are so tired. Rest, cara, rest. Tomorrow we can talk, but not tonight. Do not worry now, cara. We will take care of this, and you shall rest. We will protect you, now that we know the danger. I shall discover who is behind all this, and they shall be punished. I promise you. Tonight, you must sleep, rest. Tomorrow, you will feel much better. Yes?'

'Oh, yes, yes,' she said, thankfully.

CHAPTER 10

Veronica felt so much better she wanted to sing. Pietro did sing, and she loved to listen to him. The arsenic was no longer in her system, she felt livelier, much more interested in life, eager for what lay ahead.

Pietro hung over her, anxious, devoted. He remained with her much of the day. He followed her around when she strolled outdoors among the late flowers, the chilly petals of roses falling on their hands when they stopped to touch the last ones.

He was so tender, so gentle.

And finally he came to her bed one night,

as she tossed restlessly, awake, longing. He tapped on the door, came in at her call.

'Veronica, you are awake?' he murmured.

She stiffened with shyness, with longing and hunger. He had not touched her in love-making for so long. She had begun to wonder if he still wanted her, if his desires were dead.

'What is it, Pietro?' she asked, sitting up.

He came over to the bed, a shadow dimly seen in the room. He touched her blonde hair with his hand, his palm lingering over her forehead. 'I have wondered, darling, when you might welcome me again,' he said simply. 'I have stayed away, waiting to see if you would come to me. But my longing drives me—still I don't wish to hurt you—I don't know how you feel—'

It was a rare occasion when Pietro stammered like a boy. Her heart caught, then raced ahead faster.

She stammered in turn, shyly. 'I—I didn't want to bother—I am feeling fine now, you know that—please stay, Pietro—if—if you want to—'

She moved over as he got into bed with her. She felt hot and cold by turns as he slid down beside her, turned to her, drew up the blankets over them both. He did seem eager, his arms closed hungrily around her.

'I never know what to think with you, Veronica,' he confessed, his voice deep. 'You are so different, I can't tell what you are thinking—not about me—I don't know if you want me or not. You did not come to my bed, as I invited you.'

She rubbed her cheek against his chest. 'I—I wasn't sure you wanted me.' she said, in a low tone. 'And then—when I was ill—I couldn't seem to feel anything. I was so tired all the time, except—'

'Except—what, cara?' His voice was huskily caressing, his hand began sliding excitingly over her waist and thighs.

'Except—I wished I was well enough—that you would want—I mean—that you wanted—me—'

He bent over and caught the words from her lips, and kissed her in a deep hot kiss that smothered all other thoughts, all shyness and fears.

He whispered caressing words amidst his other more intimate caresses, and she began to burn with heat that was the most exciting she had known. He drew up her gown, pulled it off completely, and tossed it away into the darkness of the room. She felt his lips roaming warmly over her shoulders, her breasts, her arms, while his hands prepared her skilfully for his embrace.

It had been a long time since they had met like this. Their mutual hungers flowed together, built up, raced more rapidly, then flowed in a flood, overwhelming them both in a mighty torrent of emotion. She was sobbing with delight when they had finished, and he lay back on the pillow at her side.

He still held her closely, tightly. She turned to his side, and pressed her wet face against his bare chest. 'Caro, caro, my darling, my darling,' she whispered.

Her mind felt blurred with the experience. Her blood sang, her body burned and glowed with the fire. He was drawing rapid breaths, his chest rising and falling under her cheek.

'I did it too fast,' he murmured presently. 'Did I hurt you? I could not control it—'

'No, no, it was beautiful. I loved it,' she said, her lips shyly against his moist throat. She would not say yet the words she longed to say, the simple 'I love you,' that she wanted to shout aloud. She loved him, but still some reserve held her back.

She wanted him to do it again, to hold her closely, to let her know the mindless delight of flooded senses, of drowning sensuality and heat, the wild final volcano of thrills.

But he held her quietly, stroked her back,

175

encouraged her to drift off to sleep in his arms.

He was so gentle, so careful with her, always. Yet, somehow, she wanted that control to slip, to loose itself completely, with her the willing victim, the glowing partner, the delighted helpless love-object of her husband.

But he was always careful, always gentle. And he did not say that he loved her.

Only that marred her days and nights. She felt almost well again, the shoulder healed, her body recovering from the poisoning. She spent days on the balcony, evenings in their personal living room, sometimes with Pietro, sometimes with the rest of his family.

As the days grew colder, she came indoors to work at her sketching. She no longer felt like lying helplessly on a lounge chair on the balcony, watching clouds drifting past. She felt much more alert and her mind jumped from one project to another.

Camilla had brought her some books from the family library, showing beautiful ancient designs of heraldry, of flowers, of birds and insects. Veronica had been studying them until they had inspired her in some jewellery designs.

One morning as she worked on the designs, they had an unexpected conversation.

Veronica had been copying some sketches from her notebook to some design paper for the use of the shop. Pietro was sitting in one of the large armchairs in their living room, just beyond his bedroom. Veronica sat at the large mosaic-topped table, working on a sketch pad, studying the design, erasing carefully, sketching again. Sometimes she put her tongue between her teeth like a child, concentrating.

'There,' she sighed, softly, and sat back, studying it. She lifted it, held it to the light of the daylight streaming in the French windows.

'It is finished, yes?' said Pietro's deep voice, behind her. She started. She had not heard him stand up and come over to her. She handed him the finished sketch.

'Yes, this one. For the duchess and her aquamarines. Do you like that?' she added anxiously. Pietro was a personal friend of this duchess, she had learned.

He took the sketch, studied it. 'It is exquisite. She will like it immensely. They can start on it this week at the shop, I believe. What is this other one?' He bent over her shoulder, touched the sketch pad opened beside her.

'That? Oh, just an idea. I put down the ideas when I think of them. When we have a commission I look through for ideas that might suit or be adaptable.'

He turned the pages slowly, his large brown hand smoothing the pages carefully as he lifted one. She watched his fingers, blushing at her own thoughts. They had caressed her body just as carefully, as tenderly, last night. She had adored his touch. He seemed to have utmost sensitivity in his fingers, awakening sensations in her that made her want to sing and dance with joy.

He laid down the pad, and moved away slowly. She stood up and stretched. She had been sitting a long time. She smoothed out the mussed skirts of her pink muslin dress, adjusted the pink cashmere sweater around her shoulders. The room was cool.

'Come over here, cara,' he invited, sitting down on the large blue couch near the windows. She went over to sit beside him and he took her small hand in his. He seemed to want to study it, and she looked at her small white hand curiously. What did he see in that little hand, those long slim fingers?'

'You are very talented,' he said, finally. 'I am curious, Veronica. Did your father teach you to draw, to sketch, to make designs for jewellery?'

She closed her fingers slowly around his thumb that was caressing her palm. She felt very close to him, intimately involved with him, alone in their huge living room. The sunlight glanced off the marble-topped tables, the framed pictures on the walls, the plush-covered chairs of red velvet, blue velvet, the glass paperweights from Venice. The walls were covered with a delicate design in blue and white, and set off the red velvet of the window-drapes.

'I think I was born knowing how to draw,' she finally said, simply. 'I have sketched as long as I can remember. Later father had a drawing teacher for me, and in the convent school I had many art classes in painting and watercolour. I did not do any jewellery designing until later, though. When father became ill, he wanted me to work on this, and so I did, and found I liked it very much.'

'Your father encouraged your art?' he asked.

'Yes, we were alike in this, he thought. He loved his art work. He had wished to be a famous painter, but his talents lay in business, and he did not seem sorry about that. I remember how he used to touch the gem stones, the gold and silver threads, how lovingly he laid out the gems in a pattern, then scattered them and did another.'

'And you are like him. You enjoy this work,' he said. He was frowning slightly. She looked up at his darkly handsome face, wishing she could read his mind.

'Yes, I like the work, Pietro,' she said,

quietly. 'Does that disturb you? Tell me please. I wish to be—what you want me to be,' she added, blushing.

He looked down into her eyes, then smiled slightly, in pleasure. 'Do you? Thank you, cara. I have been thinking so much, I am puzzled. I told you. I do not understand you much, though I wish to do so. You said—you told me you wished for children, to be a wife and mother. And yet—this work—you seem so happy to return to it.'

Her breath caught. 'Oh, Pietro—I want both!' she cried out. 'Do you think I should choose between them? That one can have only one or the other? Is that true?'

He frowned again, thoughtfully. 'I don't know, cara. The women I know—they are either business women, or they are wives and mothers, staying home, overseeing the house, planning meals. I do not know any women who do both of these things. But you—you want both. I cannot think how this can be.'

She swallowed. The light seemed to swirl around her. Could she choose between Pietro and her love of drawing? 'Oh,—oh, please don't say that,' she whispered. 'I can't—I can't—choose! I want a child, oh, I do—and yet—'

She clutched his big hand with both of hers,

pleading for understanding, gazing up at him, studying his dark eyes passionately.

'Cara, do not be disturbed,' he said, calmly. He bent and kissed her cheek warmly. 'You are a very intelligent woman. I think you will find an answer. Just because I am a man of limited experiences and do not know much about women—'

She giggled. He stared at her.

'Oh, Pietro! How can you say that?' she gurgled, her sense of humour bursting out unexpectedly. 'You—not experienced!'

For one moment, she thought he was going to be offended. People did not often laugh at Pietro. Then his brow cleared, and he laughed also.

'So—I sound too modest, do I? My wife thinks I have had vast experiences! Well, that isn't too bad— perhaps! But, truly, cara, I think I have never met any woman like you. You are much more complicated than any lady I know.'

She thought about that, and was not sure she liked it or not. Did a man like Pietro love a complicated woman? Or did he want a calm unexciting housewife?

That was the first of several conversations they had, rather timidly, then with more freedom, exploring each other's minds and wishes. She felt she was becoming more acquainted with him, now more at ease with him.

In late November, Andy sent a note to the villa, and they soon all hurried down to the shop in Florence. Andy met them beaming, and excited.

He got the jewels from the office safe and spread them carefully on a white silk mat on his desk. Veronica gasped, Pietro stared, Giorgio clucked his tongue.

'Such pearls—such rubies!' gasped Veronica again and again. She finally dared to pick up the first heavy strand of rubies, interspersed with exquisite huge baroque pearls.

'Very bad taste,' said Giorgio, touching the mammoth tiara of pearls set with huge rubies, so heavy it must have weighed sadly on a lady's head in the evening at the ball.

'The Contessa Guilia d'Antoniazzo,' recited Andy proudly. He looked at each face in turn. 'Wow. When she walked in, and came in my office, and spilled those jewels on the desk—I just about fainted! I never saw such a lot. She said she knew your family, duke, and had heard of our designs. She said we are free to do just whatever we wish. She wants something exquisite in the modern manner.'

'I know the family,' said Pietro, nodding. 'Yes, her father was a friend of my grandfather, in the old days. I think they fought together, on the same side.'

'How much time do we have?' asked Veronica, practically. She was thinking that Andy had looked disappointed, he must have expected Camilla to come also. And he had called her husband 'duke' instead of his first name, as he had before. Had something chilled the air again, or was this still the old feud? She hated the bad feeling between Pietro and Andy. Andy still wasn't accustomed to royalty, he didn't know how to address Pietro. Poor Andy, so blunt and American, she thought, with a sigh.

'She said anytime. Then she said she wanted to wear them for a ball before Lent. That gives us—let's see—three months, at least. But we have the eight commissions from Rome, two from Venice, three from Milan.'

Some of Veronica's excitement died. She fingered the heavy baroque pearl pin thoughtfully. So much work to do. They had been almost too successful, Pietro and his men, in finding commissions. She had been working hard, and yet she was behind in her share of the designs. She knew Andy had too much to do, and was frantically trying to catch up and keep ahead of the jewellery-makers in the shop.

Who could they get to help them? They really needed another designer. But it might take years to train someone.

'If I had these gems,' said Giorgio, still holding the tiara, turning it this way and that to catch the lights, 'I'd cut up the whole thing. This setting is wrong. It should be a dainty tiara, with a single ruby centred like a flower in a thin sparkling silver frame, with a few baroque pearls like dew-drops on the wires. Take the pearls, make something else of them, a brooch, for another occasion. I would take these all apart—and that necklace! Dreadful. I would make a three or four strand dog-collar of pearls, with a ruby pendant— some special shape—I know the contessa, the symbol of their house is the little sea-serpent, with a winding tail—something like that would be charming—'

Veronica stared at him, blinking. Giorgio had shown only a mild interest in gems before. Now he rattled on as though he knew a great deal.

'Fortunately, there is time to work on this—' Pietro was saying. Veronica interrupted him, with unintentional sharpness.

'Giorgio! Why don't you plan the designs? You have a marvellous idea. Why don't you go ahead and do it? Can you draw and sketch? I'll show you how to outline them...'

Giorgio frowned down at her. He dropped

the tiara as though it burned him. 'I? I plan the designs?' he said rudely. 'I'm not in trade!'

Veronica swallowed. Pietro had turned red and ashamed. Veronica knew that Giorgio and his father had been against Pietro's venture into trade, but how else would they have lived?

'I'm sorry,' she said, coldly. 'Forgive me, Andy, let me think about this, I can...'

Andy burst out, red-faced, angry. 'In trade! What do you think we are doing, playing games? Sure we are in trade! And proud of it! We earn our living, we don't live off other people! We use our talents and earn our bread. What is wrong with that?'

Giorgio turned up his nose, sneering. It was Pietro who reacted furiously. He flung on Andy, his fists clenching.

'How dare you speak to my cousin like that? He does not need to be in trade. He is a nobleman! He can do as he wishes! You do not understand, you Americans. You don't understand how a nobleman has obligations...' He shut himself off, oddly, with a glance down at Veronica, staring up at him.

Veronica could not say a word. Andy flared back at Pietro, as though he had held back words too long.

'Nobleman! What is noble about being poor? If a man has a talent and uses it, why should others look down on him! A man is as good as another, so long as he has honour and courage!'

The two men glared at each other, uneasily. Veronica felt there was more behind this than she understood, also that the argument had gone on too long.

Pietro said, 'You do not understand Italian ways!'

'I understand honour and integrity and hard work!' Andy shot back at him.

'Integrity—are you sure you know that?' asked Pietro.

Andy looked ready to boil over. Veronica stood up, stepping between them. 'Please, no more. I am weary. Andy, please put these in the safe.' She indicated the jewels, those beautiful gems that had precipitated another quarrel. Perhaps jewels excited men and women, she thought, making them angry and troublesome, greedy and thoughtless.

Andy hesitated, then made her a strange jerky bow, his face bright red, and scooped up the jewels. He put them in their lovely velvet bags, and away into the safe. Giorgio went out into the shop to look at the display cases, as though he had become indifferent to them all.

'Pietro you said you had another commission from Pisa,' she said. 'I will discuss this with

186

Andy today. The designs for the ladies in Rome must wait for a while.' She opened her handbag, and took out her sketch pad. Her mind was whirling, with doubts, troubles, worries.

Pietro hesitated, then sat down also. He waited in silence, while she and Andy talked about the Pisan lady's wishes. 'I will work on that this week, since she wants it for Christmas,' said Veronica, finally. 'Is that the only urgent commission, Andy?'

He shrugged. 'One of the ladies in Rome said her commission was urgent. She said she was promised by the Duke d'Isola d'Oro that she should have it this month.' He flung a nasty look at Pietro.

It took a moment for Veronica to remember that this was one of Pietro's titles. The two men glared at each other again.

'That was the Duchess of Trevino's commission.' Pietro finally said quietly. 'She is always impatient. Do it when you can. There is no such rush. She will wait.' He got up and strode around the office, then went out to the shop to speak to Giorgio.

Veronica hissed at Andy, 'Why must you quarrel with him all the time? What is the matter with you?'

He did not answer this. 'He said—integrity!' Andy's hands were shaking. 'Is that why

Camilla did not come today? Is he afraid to let her look at me? To let me see her? I haven't seen her for weeks!'

Something clicked in Veronica's head, something suddenly made sense. Andy was in love, and with Camilla. She put her hand on Andy's gently. 'Patience,' she murmured. 'Wait. She is only seventeen.'

'Girls have married before then. And *he* might marry her off to a nobleman!' said Andy, with intense bitterness.

Veronica shook her head, looked up to see Pietro inside the room again. He was gazing at her hand lying on Andy's She drew it off as though it burned. She got up to leave, gathered up her sketches with shaking hands.

She didn't want Pietro to get jealous again. Yet she couldn't tell him what they were talking about. He was very prickly when it came to his beloved younger sister, and so too, thought Veronica, so too was his wife. She wanted Camilla to marry well, to marry the man she loved. No marriage of convenience for Camilla, not if Veronica could prevent it!

CHAPTER 11

Andy jumped up as Veronica came into the yellow salon. She smiled to see him.

'Andy, how nice to see you. I have more sketches for you. They were not finished when Pietro went down to Florence on his way to Rome.'

'Please, close the door,' he said softly.

Her eyebrows went up. She stared at him. 'My husband is very jealous...' she murmured.

He shook his head, impatiently. 'I have to tell you something. No one must hear.'

She hesitated visibly. 'I could call Camilla...'

'Later. She must not hear this.'

She studied his face gravely. She nodded, went back to the door, and closed it. She returned, to sit on the yellow satin sofa. He perched on the edge of the blue chair.

'When does Pietro return?' he asked.

'This evening. He arrives from Rome at...'

'Never mind. Listen. The gems of the Contessa Guilia d'Antoniazzo have disappeared.'

'Disappeared!' she repeated faintly, and her hand went to her heart. Again it was racing madly. Was there no end to her troubles? 'How—when—are you sure they...'

'They are gone, completely. I saw them in the safe two days ago, when I opened it. I delivered the gems to Pietro. Giorgio was there. They were taking the gems to Rome. I went to the shop, to speak to a client. When I returned, the safe was closed. Pietro was wrapping the gems for Rome in a cloth, and Giorgio was standing near the windows, near his cloth travelling bag. He was putting something in it.'

'Oh—my—dear—God—oh, Mary, have mercy,' Veronica was muttering, feeling terribly faint and stricken. 'They could not—no, no—they could not...'

'I don't know that they did!' he said, impatiently, rather roughly, as though afraid she would faint. 'We must consider all the possibilities. Who knows the safe combination? I do, my foreman does, you do, Pietro...'

'Giorgio, Uncle Teodosio, that is all,' she finished. She lay back against the sofa, her hand to her cheek. 'Oh, dear God. I must think. I must think. They would not. Who else could have... The foreman, would he?'

'As faithful and loyal and good-hearted as you would want,' Andy said. 'He has access to the gems constantly. He has never taken so much as a tiny pearl in all the years of working for your father. No, not him. But something must have happened. A robbery. Or perhaps Pietro has decided to design something, brought them up here to the villa.'

She shook her head slowly. 'No. We spoke of the Contessa's gems just before he left on this journey. I asked him to bring them up to the villa, and I would design for them. He refused, angrily. He said I was working too hard. He said that—that Andy Kelly must do more, that it was his job to do the Contessa's gems. We quarrelled. Camilla was upset, and wept.' She wiped her palm slowly over her forehead. brushing back the damp blonde curls that clung there. 'Oh, dear God, who, who is doing this to us?'

'I don't know. What do you want me to do? You're the boss, the head of Murray's,' he said, crisply. He sounded hard and businesslike, toughened from the cheerful friend he had been. 'You must make the decisions.'

Her backbone stiffened. She sat up straight, smoothed her skirts, put aside her troubles to think.

'We must not let this news out. It must be secret,' she said, with more assurance. 'If people learn their gems are not safe with us, we shall lose all the goodwill we have earned over the years. Keep it secret for a time. Give me time to plan. The police? No, they must not be told yet. It would go straight to the Contessa. Let me think.' She rubbed her face again.

'You could ask Pietro. Ask if he has taken the gems.'

'No, no, I cannot do that! He must tell me first,' she cried out passionately. 'I cannot hurt Pietro...'

The door burst open. Pietro blew into the room like a gusty winter wind. He glared at them incredulously, raged like a volcano.

'What is this? You two again? Veronica, how can you be so cruel and heartless? Did you not know the servants would talk? Andy, you must leave us! Leave Florence! You go too far! To seduce my wife in our own home! How much do you think a man will endure? Go! Go!'

Andy came raging to his feet, bursting with fury. 'You stupid bastard! How can you so insult me and your wife? I would never seduce her! We were talking of business...'

'Yes, yes, I see that! Always business—and you cannot tell Pietro—you cannot hurt Pietro—' He was sneering at Veronica now.

He had heard just enough to misunderstand. Andy glared at him, looked at Veronica who was rising slowly from the yellow sofa. She felt so small, so helpless, but her voice was firm.

'Pietro, you will apologize to Andy Kelly,' she said, coldly. 'He does not deserve such terms. He is here as my guest, as my employee. He did come on business, you must believe that.' She held her head high, met his stare fully.

Pietro's dark face turned darker red. 'Apologize?' he bellowed. 'For not having time to seduce you? How much must a man take from you, his wife?'

She was chilled, but steady. Her hands clasped together. 'Without trust, there is nothing,' she said. She turned to Andy, hoping he would comprehend that her words had a double meaning. She had decided to trust Pietro. 'Andy, thank you for coming. I will take care of the matter. You may leave now.'

Andy nodded, brushed past Pietro who glared at him, stepped aside slowly. The salon door slammed after him. Pietro's voice raised in rage, in fury at his wife.

She stood silently a few moments, then went out of the room, leaving him to shout after her.

No one was there in the hallway except Giorgio, slowly climbing the stairs, glancing back curiously toward her. He carried a cloth travelling case, the same one he had taken on the trip. Veronica wished she dared challenge the man to open the case.

193

She could not, of course. If Giorgio had decided to steal the gems, there was nothing she could do about it. It would be hopeless, the business Frank Murray had painfully built up would be bankrupt.

She went up to her room, to rest, and pray, and ponder over the heavy weight in her heart.

She was sitting quietly as Pietro burst into the room.

'We have not finished talking,' he said ominously.

She braced herself for the storm of words. There was nothing else she could do. She could not tell him the truth, confess the horrible concern in her mind.

CHAPTER 12

After a long bitter quarrel, Pietro turned cold to Veronica, scarcely spoke to her. She in turn felt that it was his place to apologize for his insults to her and to Andy.

They slept, each in his own bed, each in his own room, ate at opposite ends of the long dining room table. They spoke only of the business, and not much about that.

Camilla was hurt, bewildered, like a puppy running from one to the other, trying to make peace.

'He does not trust me,' Veronica explained once to her. 'How can he have lived with me and not trusted me! No, I will explain nothing to him! He has insulted me seriously.'

Tears dripped from the girl's eyes and rolled down her pink cheeks. 'But Veronica, but Veronica, dearest sister...'

'No, he must apologize. Or better yet, let me alone! I have work to do,' she said, then at once hugged Camilla. 'No, no, I don't mean it. You are one dear friend, the only one I have. Don't leave me. We will straighten this out eventually. But why is he so jealous and unreasonable?'

'Because he loves you deeply,' said Camilla sweetly, earnestly.

Veronica caught her breath, almost spoke out passionately, caught the words back. No, she did not think Pietro loved her.

'Do you think—does Andy Kelly—does Mr Kelly—' Camilla began, stammering, after a pause. 'Does he—does he imagine himself in love with you?'

'No,' said Veronica, flatly, a swift glance at Camilla's innocent-guilty crimson face confirming a suspicion. 'He does not love me. We are friends. He is a good strong friend, who will help me any way he can. I told you what he did concerning my father.'

'Yes, yes, but surely no man would do such a thing unless—' Camilla trembled between doubt and her desire to be certain.

'Unless he is a good friend, who is strong and courageous, and doesn't care what people think,' said Veronica, very firmly. 'He has proved himself a true friend. I am all the angrier at Pietro that he cannot see this.'

But in her calmer moments, she acknowledged that the circumstances had looked strange. And to an Italian, jealous, quick-tempered, suspicious anyway, the closed door of the salon, their conversation must have looked like a love affair. She told herself that she ought to confront him with the theft of the gems. That should convince him they had spoken of business! But inside herself was a small doubt that nagged and would not be quieted. What if Pietro had taken the gems, or Giorgio had taken them with Pietro's knowledge?

Over and over, she considered the facts. Only a certain few persons had the combination of the safe. Only a few persons were in that office when the safe was open. No outsider could possibly have stolen inside and taken the gems.

Also, not all the gems in the safe had been

stolen. Only the gems of the Contessa d'Antoniazzo were gone. Not the other gems, equally valuable, the loose stones, the jewels lying in their little boxes waiting to be reset. Only the Contessa's gems were gone, the enormous rubies, the baroque pearls. No outside thief would have been so careful to choose only the packages that contained the Contessa's gems.

To replace them would cost her entire fortune, the fortune that was not even legally hers as yet. Her birthday was in May, and she would be twenty-one. Until that time, she was helpless to act. She could not hope to confess to the Contessa and promise to give her the value in return.

And if the word leaked out, as it was sure to do, the theft would cut off their thriving business immediately. No one would trust Murray's with their precious jewels.

Worrying did no good. Veronica turned to her work with relief. She sketched all day, into the evening sometimes, until the daylight had faded and the evening lamps were lighted in the yellow salon. Then she went upstairs and prepared for dinner, wearing one of her most attractive dresses.

She knew why she consciously chose the most attractive dress. Why she smoothed her blonde hair carefully, wore it in the most attractive upsweep, sometimes put on her pearls even to dinner at home. She wanted Pietro to look at her, to find her attractive, to want her, to desire her, to come to her—no matter how jealous and suspicious he was.

But he would look at her with his hurt brown eyes, turn to Camilla or Giorgio, or Uncle Teodosio, and speak only to them, not to her, except in the most cold and formal tones.

He was exasperating!

Perhaps he was regretting the Italian beauty, she thought one evening in the salon after dinner. She was wearing her green brocade with the emerald and pearl necklace and bracelet. She was seated on the yellow satin sofa, and Camilla had told her how breathtakingly lovely she looked. Camilla herself wore her most charming blue silk dress, and Veronica wished that Andy could see her now, relaxed and lovely in her home, the pretty girl who was her sister. Andy would be more smitten with Camilla than ever!

But Pietro had turned deliberately from them, staring into the fire blazing in the huge marble fireplace. He was silent, drinking his coffee, thinking his own brooding thoughts.

Perhaps he saw the dark beauty, Regina Ruggeri, in those flames, thought Veronica. Maybe he regretted marrying the blonde aggressive business-woman, the American woman.

There were only two activities they really shared now. One was the jewellery business. She consulted with him regularly about the designs, the orders. She went to Florence with him once a week, sitting silently in the carriage all the way down and back, to talk to Andy with Pietro sitting there near them glaring and brooding and angry.

The orders were coming along well. Andy marvelled aloud that she had the time and patience and genius to come up with such wonderful designs. And Pietro only glared at him. He had little praise for her, and that was reluctant and stiff. 'Yes, that design will please the duchess,' he would say. 'Yes, the colours are good, the exquisite slimness of the bracelet will flatter her arm.'

Veronica made a face at herself. She wanted Pietro to praise her, to flatter her, she admitted. She wanted him to look at her with desire, to love her as a woman, to admire her as a designer and an artist. And he didn't even look at her!

And they had little else in common except their rides. Each morning since her recovery, they had ridden horseback together, down the winding lanes near the Villa d'Oro. Sometimes they rode as far uphill as they wanted, toward

Fiesole, then when the horses tired, they turned and came down again, riding for two hours.

At first, they had ridden close together, talking sometimes, or riding in companionable silence that was closer than words.

After the quarrel, the rides were completely in silence, except for a few words of direction to their horses! But Veronica would not have given up the rides for anything in the world, she thought. It was the only time she was completely alone with Pietro. Even the grooms did not ride with them.

Sometime, he would have to give in, she thought. He would, he must, break out of this cold shell and apologize for his suspicions, and trust her.

But he said nothing.

And the weeks went on and on.

It was coming towards Christmas. Camilla and Veronica had attended the small nearby church, and had had the priest come to give Mass in their chapel. Pietro attended with them, sitting behind them with Giorgio and his uncle.

Veronica wondered about Christmas, presents, a tree. It was not the custom in Italy to have a tree, Camilla finally explained to her. Presents were given to children early in January, at Epiphany. Adults sometimes exchanged gifts, though, and she wanted to give something to Veronica, if Veronica would approve.

Veronica, lonely at Christmas, hungry for the bright holiday season in New York, starved for the affection her husband was denying her, approved of the gifts. On her next trip to Florence, she went shopping with Camilla and the maid, firmly leaving Pietro behind in the shop.

She would buy gifts for all of them, even the cynical Giorgio, she thought. They would learn the independent American woman in their midst was going to celebrate Christmas, whether they did or not!

The weather grew colder, the skies were grey as they started out on horseback one morning. Veronica had her favourite horse, a placid grey, elderly and calm and non-startling. She was not a great horse-woman, and preferred not to gallop along, just to ride quietly, enjoying the day.

Pietro was on his taller black stallion, his favourite. He did look stunning, she thought, in his black riding habit, his shiny black boots, the dark hair free to blow in the wind. He wore a yellow scarf around his neck, the only note of colour.

Her riding outfit was blue velvet, trailing

over her grey boots. She rode side-saddle, hooking her knee over the saddle, facing forward.

The groom said, as he helped her up, 'It might storm today, Signora.'

'We will not ride long then,' she said. 'I suppose the storms will come more often now that it is December.'

'Oh, yes, there will be maybe some snow this winter,' he assured her cheerfully, his black eyes sparkling. He smiled as she thanked him, and stood back from the horse.

Her usually placid horse started off nervously, his feet seemingly uncertain on the path. She patted his neck, spoke soothingly as they went out the gate. Pietro was slightly behind her.

He caught up with her as the lane widened.

'You spoke to your horse in Italian, Veronica,' he said, with the first approval in his tone she had noted in weeks.

'I did? Oh, yes, I did!' she said. 'I hadn't realized. It is becoming natural for me.'

'That is good. Which way shall we go today?'

She pointed down the lane with her whip. 'That way. It is shorter. Then if it does storm we shan't be far.' Her horse shied nervously, she patted his neck again. 'What is the matter with you, Patriot? Do you smell the storm coming?'

'He probably does,' said Pietro. 'My horse is nervous also. Come on, now, come along! Stop that!' He soothed his horse, his gloved hand stroking along the neck.

But the horses remained nervous, shying at every hedge, snorting nervously, almost angrily, Veronica thought. She glanced up at the sky. It was becoming dark and overcast, with a black storm cloud covering the eastern sky.

'Look there, Pietro—' She pointed with her whip. 'How dark it is becoming.'

'We have time for a ride. That will not come for another hour,' he said.

They jogged along in silence. The wind was chill, but her riding habit was warm and comfortable. She did not know why her uneasiness was growing. She kept glancing at every hedge, every tree. Did she feel she was watched? Was something wrong? A strong intuitive warning was jangling her nerves. There was trouble somewhere. She could not find the direction it was coming from, but she knew it was there.

The horses felt it, their heads kept jerking restlessly at the bits. They rode slowly, side by side, Pietro kept looking about also, his eyebrows drawn in a dark frown of worry.

'What is it,' she began. 'Pietro—'

A scream, eerie and blood-curdling, broke into her quiet voice. Her horse reared, Pietro's bounded up, and turned clear around. He was fighting to calm it when her horse took off and began racing along the lane, blindly, wild with fright. She tried to pull it back, but her arms were not strong enough. It had the bit between its teeth, and fright drove it madly.

A hedge reared in front of her. The horse dodged it, then met another headlong. Veronica felt like screaming. But the scream would only frighten her horse further. She pulled, till her arms hurt. The horse met another hedge, and instead of ploughing through it, he jumped.

She felt herself slipping, sliding. She managed to get her foot and knee free, and fell.

She fell awkwardly, right on an elbow. Pain shot through her, blacking out her fright. Greying, blacking, until she was out cold. Everything was gone. She felt nothing at all, for a timeless interval.

She came to, to find herself with her head on Pietro's legs. He was stroking her cheeks slowly, bending over, touching her tenderly.

'Cara, cara, cara,' he was whispering.

She felt warm and cared for, tenderly loved. Oh, this was lovely, her mind said. Pain. What was pain? Only a stabbing in her arm. Pietro was there, he wasn't angry any more.

'Cara, cara. Her eyes flickered,' he said to someone.

'Padron, I have the horses. There is something under the saddles,' said the voice of one of the grooms. 'It is—they are pins, Signore. Pins! They dig into the horses' backs—they bleed now—No wonder they run away!'

Another man spoke, the young serious butler. 'Here—we'll get the saddles off, they won't be easy—Giovanni, help me—stupid one, get them off—'

Giorgio's crisp voice spoke with authority. His tone was short, as though he was breathless. Veronica opened her eyes. Giorgio stood near them, looking at Pietro's black stallion, soothing him with his hands while he looked at the bare back of the horse. She saw blood running thinly down the sides.

'Pins, yes. They were inserted in the saddle, in such a way that when the horses began to run the pins would dig in. Devilish! Who would hurt horses in such a way? Who saddled these horses?'

The groom spoke. He looked frightened and bewildered, Veronica thought. 'I saddled them, I confess it. But I saw nothing at that time. I brought them around to the front of the villa, I waited for the duke and duchess to come out...'

Pietro interrupted them. 'Giorgio, help me with Veronica. I think her arm is broken.'

Now pain stabbed through her as he touched her arm. She gasped. 'Oh, Pietro—that hurts—'

'Lie still, cara. Again, it happens, uh?' he added strangely. 'Well, we shall discover—lie still, cara. Giorgio, what do you think?'

Giorgio knelt beside her left arm, touched it carefully, moved it. She wanted to scream, but bit her lips till they hurt also to stifle a cry.

Giorgio said, 'Not broken. Thank God. Not broken. But I think it pains her, eh, sister?' He smiled at her kindly, the first nice smile she had had from him. 'Poor one. Always the injuries you have. But I think this one is a sprain. We will carry you back to the villa.'

'It would be better to get the carriage,' said Pietro. 'She will not be hurt so much.'

The groom and butler took the injured horses back to the villa. Giorgio remained near them, alertly, his narrowed dark eyes watching the hedges. Veronica was puzzled, then she remembered that blood-curdling scream that had startled the horses into running.

She said to Pietro, who still held her on his lap, 'Who was it that screamed, and frightened the horses? Did you see?'

He shook his head, his dark eyes shuttered.

'No, I was too busy settling my horse. Then I saw yours was running away with you and I started after you. My horse became wilder and wilder. He finally threw me also.' He added this ruefully, his pride hurt too, she could see. The dust on his coat and trousers testified to the accident.

'But someone was there, behind the hedge—'

'Yes, cara, I know.' He soothed her with his hand stroking her cheek. 'Our enemies are still around, I think,' he added, rather fiercely.

And she realized that Giorgio was keeping his hand on his knife-hilt.

The groom and butler arrived, driving the carriage. Giorgio and Pietro lifted her in, and drove back to the villa with her. The doctor was called, but it was some hours before he could arrive. Camilla soothed her with hot compresses, hot tea and sympathetic words. Pietro and Giorgio were muttering together with Uncle Teodosio.

Veronica wished Pietro would come back and stroke her face and head once more. But he left her to Camilla.

The doctor finally arrived in late afternoon, just after she had drifted off to an uneasy sleep. They wakened her for his attentions, and he pronounced his verdict at length.

The arm was sprained, not broken. She must

207

wear a sling and bandages for a time. Hot compresses, and quiet.

She agreed with the latter verdict. She was quite shaken by this new evidence that her enemies and Pietro's were not stopped at all. Someone had deliberately set the pins in their saddles. Someone had screamed, to set the horses to running and increase their pain so they would be thrown.

Only a miracle had caused her to land on soft grass and not on the hard rocks of the lane. And a miracle had allowed her to unhook her foot and knee from the saddle, so she was not dragged by the terrified horse.

She no longer felt safe outdoors. She let herself be pampered by Camilla, and the maids, who kept her inside, bathed her, fed her tea and soft foods for a while, like an invalid.

Pietro went down to Florence the next day, and was gone a long time.

He went to Rome later in the week, and came back looking grim and angry. He would not tell even Camilla what he was doing.

Veronica tried to get information from Camilla, but the girl was as puzzled as she was.

'Why did he go to Rome? The next jewellery is not ready yet,' Veronica asked her.

Camilla shrugged, her hands wide, her eyes opened to their fullest expressive width.

'Does he tell me anything? No. He talked only to Giorgio.'

'Why didn't Giorgio go with him? He should be protected, not go alone,' said Veronica, shifting uncomfortably on the couch.

Camilla shrugged again. 'He took the butler with him. He is young and strong. I think he wanted Giorgio here to protect you—or us. I don't know. I'm not supposed to go out for awhile.'

Veronica stared at her, tried to question her further. But Camilla knew little more.

Why was Pietro concerned with protecting Camilla also? Veronica had thought the 'enemy' was after her alone. Or perhaps after her and her husband Pietro. Was he after Camilla also? Who was this mysterious enemy?

She was weary of the mystery, weary of the worry, tired and wanting very badly to lean her head on Pietro's shoulder and leave everything to him. She was—frankly-scared.

The mystery was growing larger, involving more and more people. The enemy seemed everywhere, in New York, on the ship, now in Florence. There was no sanctuary anywhere, not even in the large lovely Villa d'Oro, her new home, her beloved home.

Veronica decided that for the present she would remain quietly in the villa, and design jewellery. It was the only thing she seemed able to do well, and successfully.

She felt a failure as a wife, a miserable failure at solving the mystery of the strange attacks on her. Pietro had turned away from her. Andy was kept from her.

Only in her work, could she feel at ease.

And even that was threatened—if they didn't find the stolen gems of the contessa.

CHAPTER 13

Veronica had almost forgotten the presence of Diana Jansson. Diana was remaining in Florence, had taken an apartment in a town house, and was comfortably settled, she reported happily on a visit.

Veronica had not invited her to come to the villa, but Diana and her deaf aunt appeared one day shortly before Christmas.

When Diana saw Veronica sitting propped up in a chair, her left arm in a black silk sling, she gave a little scream. She came running into the room, flung herself on her knees before Veronica.

'My darling child, what in the world has

happened now?' She was staring with wide greenish-grey eyes at the sling, at the still vivid bruise on Veronica's forehead.

'A riding accident,' said Veronica. 'It is nothing, Diana. I am just unlucky.'

'Unlucky!' Diana gasped. 'Oh, my dearest—' She stopped abruptly, significantly, as Camilla came into the room with the ponderous Aunt Emily. 'Can't we talk alone?' she added in a whisper.

Veronica glanced involuntarily at Camilla, saw by the sudden flush and hurt look that Camilla had overheard. She could have hit Diana for her thoughtlessness.

The three talked for a few minutes. Aunt Emily Jansson put her ear trumpet to her ear, leaned forward, but obviously could hear nothing of the conversation.

Finally Camilla said, 'Perhaps I could take Miss Jansson to see the flowers in the greenhouse, the lemon trees and the limes. Would she like that?'

Diana said, 'Yes, she would,' and told her aunt loudly what she was to do.

Aunt Emily nodded placidly, and went away with Camilla.

'There, now we can talk, darling,' said Diana, sitting down again beside Veronica. She leaned forward confidentially. 'Now tell me

211

exactly what has happened to you,' she said, as imperiously as in the old days at the convent school.

Veronica studied the lovely strong-willed girl. She smiled. 'Just an accident, Diana,' she lied smoothly. It was none of Diana's business what happened to her, she thought. Perhaps her stay in Italy was making her secretive, but she was acquiring the feeling that too many people knew her concerns. 'Pietro and I were out riding, my horse took fright and ran with me. I'm a poor horsewoman, you know, and I fell.'

'Just as you fell on the ship?' asked Diana singificantly. 'No, darling, I don't believe it. You're too trusting. Where was Pietro when you fell?'

'Coming to my rescue,' said Veronica. She laughed. 'Come, now, Diana, don't make something of nothing.' She felt cold and frightened herself, she didn't want any sympathy from Diana, any more warnings. Pietro would take care of everything.

'I can't help worrying,' said Diana. 'Listen, darling, forgive me for coming like this. I know now it isn't done in Italy, to come right up to the villa and barge in. But I had to tell you about your husband, about Pietro.'

The greenish-grey eyes were watching for her reaction. Veronica schooled herself to stiffness,

212

hoping her face would not give her away.

'I don't care to hear idle gossip, Diana. Now tell me what you plan to do over Christmas. Are you going up to London, as you thought?'

Her attempt to change the subject was unsuccessful.

'No, I'm not, I'm going to stay right here,' said the blonde girl firmly. She nodded her golden head decisively. 'Veronica, I have heard gossip, and I must tell you. Pietro has been very poor—before your marriage. I think you know that. He married you for the money, that is well-known. Now he is buying heavily. I've heard he has bought a fortune in gems, and is considering opening the palazzo on the Golden Isle, the one he still owns.'

The shock of it caught at Veronica's breath. She could not conceal her surprise and dismay. Diana nodded

'Yes, it's true. He has talked to some friends about opening the palazzo. And I saw myself the gems he is purchasing. Don't ask me how —I have made it my concern to find out whatever concerns my trusting little friend!' She patted Veronica's hand, exclaimed, 'But your hand is cold, darling! Oh, dear, I've shocked you too much! I'm too blunt!'

'No, no, it's all right.' Veronica withdrew her hand, slowly enough not to insult Diana.

213

The big warm hand of the older girl had felt sympathetic, and she did not want to give way to tears. 'Don't listen to people, Diana, they don't know the truth.'

'But I must listen!' She lowered her voice to a murmur, watched Veronica's face keenly as she went on. 'Darling, I have met the woman he loves! Her name is Regina Ruggeri. He has been with her frequently of late. She brags that he has returned to her, tired of his meek American wife...'

Now a knife did turn in Veronica's heart. She remembered vividly the proud dark beauty in the box at the Pergola Theatre.

'I'm sorry, dear. But you must have known about her. All Florence is talking...'

Veronica drew herself up proudly. She forced the words through stiff lips. 'Then all Florence must be desperate for a topic of conversation. No, no more, Diana. I won't listen to you. Tell me your Christmas plans—and what do you hear from New York City—'

Diana would not change the subject. Relentlessly, she poured out the gossip, eagerly, as though unable to comprehend how much she was hurting her friend.

'You must know about this. No American woman would put up with such scandalous behaviour. He has bought gems for her, a rope of pearls, a pendant of emeralds. You'll see the jewels yourself. She plans to wear them to the next concert, whatever opera you and Pietro attend! All Florence knows of your rivalry.'

'Please, Diana! Stop it, I won't listen.' She tried to put her hands over her ears, but the left arm pained her too much to move it.

'He is spending a great deal of money. Where does he get it? Does he have access to your fortune already? I had a letter from your stepmother, she is terribly concerned about you. The attack in Florence, I wrote her about it, how ill you were. She told me she was afraid Pietro might...'

'Stop it!' Veronica pulled herself to her feet. 'Stop it at once. I will not listen!' Her eyes blazed at Diana. 'I won't listen to such vile remarks! You had no right to communicate with my stepmother concerning me! I trust my husband, I will not listen to such talk about him.'

Diana tried to speak again. She had risen, and towered over tiny Veronica. She tried to dominate the girl, but Veronica would have none of it.

'No, no, don't speak again. Please go! This is Pietro's house, I won't have you in it if you speak like this!'

'He has bewitched you,' said Diana sorrowfully, and tears came into her eyes.

Veronica had to laugh in spite of her fury. 'Bewitched! Diana, you are too old-fashioned,' she taunted her, knowing that alone could send Diana into a fury. Diana liked to think she was ultra-modern.

Diana bit her lips, the full red mouth straightening. But tears still gemmed her eyes. 'He has done something, drugged you, changed you. I don't know what. But Sybil is afraid he will try to kill you for your money. Veronica, come back to America. I'll take you back. You don't have to endure such misery...'

'Don't be ridiculous,' said Veronica, calming suddenly. Diana was being dramatic as usual. She had always loved play-acting. 'Pietro and I are very fond of each other. Of course, he is spending money. The villa needed fixing up. We are planning to change all the drapes in the place. They are really falling apart in places. Come now, Diana, be calm. Visit with me, and tell me the New York news.'

She sat down again, in command of herself once more. The foolish charge that Pietro would kill her had quieted her, made her see how ridiculous Diana's charges were. She knew about Regina Ruggeri, how much Pietro despised her. He would never become her lover again. He could have married her, and had

216

refused to do so. No, Pietro liked Veronica, and she had some hope that someday he would come to love her.

Diana seemed to struggle with herself, and finally sat down again reluctantly.

'I wish you would listen to my warning,' she began again.

'No, I won't. Now, tell me about the opera last week. We missed it. Was the Divine Soprano marvellous, or just ordinary?'

Diana sighed heavily. 'Oh, she was all right,' she said. 'The tenor was terribly heavy, and looked awful. I had to close my eyes to retain my illusions. And everyone around me had eaten garlic for supper,' she added, so unhappily that Veronica burst out laughing.

She was still laughing when Camilla and Aunt Emily Jansson returned. Camilla looked intensely relieved to see Veronica laughing.

'We were discussing the opera,' said Veronica, looking at Camilla significantly.

They managed to keep the conversation on opera, concerts, flowers, until Diana and her aunt had left.

But after they had left. Diana's words came back again and again. Pietro was buying heavily. He had bought a rope of pearls and an emerald pendant. For whom? Perhaps he had bought it for herself for Christmas, she thought, and felt a little lift of spirits. Maybe, maybe—

But Diana got the gossip all mixed up, probably, she reminded herself. She was overly dramatic, living in a strange country she didn't understand.

Yet—Pietro had frankly married Veronica for her money, she knew that. It had been a financial arrangement, so much settled on Pietro in dowry. And he knew that Veronica would inherit the entire jewellery business when she was twenty-one in May. It had been a business arrangement between them. When her father had died, he would not hear to putting off the wedding, but Pietro had insisted on going through with the wedding.

Could it be?

No, no, of course not, thought Veronica. She ate a lonely supper with Camilla. Pietro was late in returning from Florence, and Giorgio and his uncle had gone with him. Pietro had been so cool to her lately..

He spent long hours away from her. He had gone to Rome twice, and only once was on the company business matters.

Veronica began to dread the coming of Christmas. It arrived on a cold grey morning. She lay in her huge bed, staring out at the dark bay, and could have cried. She had wrapped presents for each of them, for Pietro, Camilla, the others. Even presents for the servants. She had given them all to Maria, to put downstairs in the yellow salon.

What if they laughed at her for her sentiment, giving presents to adults? Now she began to regret what she had done. She was living in Italy now. She should live as an Italian lived. It was foolish to insist on presents, on Christmas celebrations.

She felt so lonely she wanted to stay in her room and hide. She couldn't.

She got up, washed and dressed in a green silk that felt a little festive. At home, she would have rushed from her room, run downstairs, kissed her father, laughed happily at the pile of presents under the tree.

But her father was dead. And Sybil had dampened their 'childish' interest in Christmas, even in the years her father was still alive.

Maria knocked on the door. Veronica realized she had not brought her coffee. She opened the door. The young maid beamed at her.

'Cafe in the yellow salon, Signora,' she said happily, in Italian.

Veronica walked down the long marble stairway, and heard the voices in the salon before she arrived. Her curiosity and expectations aroused, she went to the opened door and stared inside.

The first thing she saw was the tree—the oddest Christmas tree she had ever seen. It was a potted lemon tree, with a few small lemons on it. And a few small gay presents hanging from it! And next she saw Camilla's hopeful wistful face!

'Oh—oh, a Christmas tree!' laughed Veronica. She ran forward and hugged the girl. 'A Christmas tree—'

'It isn't like the American ones,' Camilla began to apologize. 'We couldn't find one, and no decorations, it is a poor thing...'

'No, no, it is a Christmas tree! How lovely! Thank you! How good of you all—' She began to realize they were all there, Camilla, Pietro, Giorgio, Uncle Teodosio, the house servants.

Pietro and Giorgio insisted that she should sit down while they gave out the gifts to the servants. She and Camilla drank their coffee. She looked as eagerly as a child at the pile of presents around the tree, hanging from the tree.

The servants thanked them, and left, closing the doors after them. Then Pietro began handing out the gifts. First, to Veronica, a huge package, very heavy, that filled her lap.

Giorgio was watching her reactions with a big smile on his face. He began to tease, in his

220

cynical manner to which she was just becoming accustomed.

'You had better like your present, dear Veronica! Pietro has dragged me to Rome a dozen times, we have scoured the shops of Florence, Milan, I thought we would have to go to England or America...'

Pietro was turning very red with embarrassment. 'Shut up, you stupid Giorgio,' he muttered. 'It isn't so—we went to Rome on business...'

Giorgio just laughed. All of them were watching her open the huge package. Finally Camilla had to help her, because she was so awkward with her sprained left arm. The paper finally came off, and a huge leather-bound book appeared.

She stared at the title, 'Flora of Italy,' it said. What a strange gift she thought, puzzled. Why had Pietro looked and looked—Then she opened the book, and began leafing through the pages, and understood.

It was filled with marvellous drawings and sketches of the flowers of Italy, beautiful flowers, named, some of the pictures coloured with the exquisite paintings that were like medieval manuscripts. She gasped again and again at their beauty, her imagination stirring.

'Oh—oh—this is so lovely. Oh, Pietro, thank

you! This will give me so many ideas for jewellery designs...' She looked at him shyly, directly, to see his face red now with pleasure and relief that she liked his gift. 'This is just what I would have wanted—if I had realized! I needed more inspiration for designs...'

'He had to pay high for it, the contessa didn't want to part with it,' said Giorgio, in high spirits.

Pietro tried to shush him, then reluctantly confessed he had found nothing he liked in the bookstores. 'I finally saw the very book in the home of a contessa in Milan. We struck a bargain. She sold me the book, and we must have a glorious set of gems for her by May.' He grimaced. 'I am afraid you, Veronica, will be the one paying for the book! It is too bad.' He tried to pass it off.

She stroked the heavy leather covers of the beautiful bound volume. He had gone to a great deal of trouble to get this for her, and he had done it because he understood her! This was the finest gift he could have given her, she thought, wishing she could jump and kiss him for it.

'Thank you very much,' she finally said, and it felt inadequate.

Pietro had handed a small gift to Camilla, who opened it and exclaimed happily over the small strand of pearls. 'He promised me pearls for my eighteenth birthday, and that is not yet for eight months!' she said. She did kiss her brother affectionately. Veronica felt jealous for a moment.

Other gifts were exchanged and opened and talked about, as they drank their morning coffee and ate sweet rolls. Giorgio seemed quite pleased with his fine fishing rod. Veronica and Camilla had been very puzzled how to choose one for him, but he seemed to approve of their choice.

She watched Pietro's face as he opened one of her gifts to him, gold cuff-links and matching stud set with good pearls. She had designed them herself. He did like them, she knew, then, and was relieved and happy.

To Camilla, she had given a long length of silk, for a pink and pearl evening gown and matching cape of black velvet lined with pink silk. Camilla squealed like a child over it.

Finally Pietro laid in Veronica's lap a small square box, and stood over her as she opened it. She exclaimed in surprise. It was a bracelet she herself had designed, with exquisite gold links, a gold design filled with rubies, shaped like a series of feathers.

'I had them make it up for you, it was too pretty to sell,' he said, quietly. 'I hope you will not be angry.'

'No, no, not angry,' she said, breathlessly. 'It is lovely, thank you, Pietro.' She tried to clasp the bracelet on her arm, but fumbled. He took it in his hands, studied the clasp, then put in on her, his fingers lingering on her smooth white arm.

Later they had breakfast, then Veronica returned to the yellow salon. She did not want to work, but she sat at her huge work desk, a mahogany table set with marble inlay, and studied her new present, the huge book of floral designs.

She kept looking at the odd Christmas tree, the small potted tree hung with lemons which shone in the huge yellow room. What a thoughtful thing for Camilla to do, knowing her sister was homesick!

And they had all been kind to her, exchanging presents, though Uncle Teodosio said out loud once that he felt like a child. He had not refused his presents, though, she thought with a little grin. He had been pleased with his scarf, his smoking jacket, his pipe.

She wondered if Pietro would like his dressing robe of black velvet trimmed with gold designs. If he would wear it. If she would ever see him in it.

He had not come to her room when she was

alone, since the quarrel over Andy. She sighed a little over the book, her fingers stroking the heavy vellum of the pages.

He had been so cool to her. Did he regret their marriage? Surely, surely, Diana had been wrong. Pietro would not turn to Regina Ruggeri, would not buy pearls and rubies for her. But—but she had not received a long rope of pearls and a pendant of emeralds from him!

Did she believe Diana, or did she not? She did not know. Seeds of doubt had been planted in her, she wanted to rip them out before they could grow.

She stared sightlessly at a glorious page of yellow roses, delicately painted with gold paint, and green and blue and red around the borders.

Half truth could be more dangerous than whole lie, she thought. Everyone probably knew that Pietro had married her for money and the business. And they also knew she had been married to him for his title and position.

Why did it have to be that way, she thought, loneliness and wistfulness creeping into her. If only she could have met Pietro under different circumstances, come to know him, love him, want to marry him. And if he could have come to love her—

But the world wasn't like that, not for the wealthy, she thought. It was too bad, but her situation had placed her here. She would have to make the best of it.

Quietly, she closed the book, and went up to her bedroom and closed the door. She didn't want to see anyone, or have them see her crying at Christmas. She lay down on the lounge chair, closed her eyes, took deep breaths to keep from weeping.

Her arm ached a little. She put her right hand on it, held it carefully, lifting the elbow to relieve the strain of the sling. She saw again the lovely golden and ruby bracelet that Pietro had given her.

She gazed at it, and her eyes blurred with tears. She lifted her arm to her lips, kissed the bracelet.

He had thought of her, he had. He had chased all over Italy to find that book for her. He had thought ahead to plan the bracelet for her, and arranged secretly to have it made up. He must have done that two months ago.

Maybe—maybe he did love her.

'But Sybil is afraid he will try to kill you for your money.'

Diana's words came echoing back to her, in Diana's strong positive tones. Diana had been truly worried and upset about her. She really believed that Veronica was in danger.

Camilla tapped at the door, and entered,

freely, as she had come to do lately. 'Darling? The priest has come for our Mass. Pietro arranged to have it in the chapel. Oh, do you feel all right?' She rushed over to Veronica. 'Is your arm paining you?'

Veronica brushed away the tears, smiled away the concern. 'It pains me a little. No, I'm all right. Please get my cloak, Camilla, will you?'

'But if you aren't feeling well...'

'I'm all right.' She stood up, and Camilla settled the cloak around her shoulders and the hood over her head. 'Don't say anything to Pietro, he will only worry,' she added, in a low tone.

Camilla nodded. 'He will go crazy,' she said, serenely. 'When you are hurt, he goes mad. After Mass, I will fix some hot compresses. We won't tell Pietro, he gets so crazy.'

That thought comforted Veronica! She went downstairs, and out to the small chapel behind the villa, and knelt on the hard bench, and prayed during the lovely Christmas Mass. She prayed for faith, for courage, for belief in Pietro, and added a little wistful prayer that he would come to love her someday.

CHAPTER 14

Winter had finally arrived in Florence, and a few cold gusts of wind and a flurry of snow flakes emphasized its arrival. Veronica was glad enough to stay quietly in the villa, working on designs.

Pietro made one trip to Rome, and the rest of the time worked in Florence. The workshop was busier than ever, filling the many orders he had gathered on his trips.

Giorgio wanted to attend the opera, and finally went with his father. Camilla pleaded to go with them, but was firmly refused. Pietro still thought they were in danger, and argued with Giorgio several times, in their passionate Italian voices like grand opera.

They received few guests. All Italy seemed to have settled down for a cold though brief winter.

Veronica was doubly surprised one morning when the young butler came to her and said that 'An American lady wishes to see the duchess.'

'An American lady?' she asked in Italian. 'Is

it the blonde lady, Miss Jansson? You know the lady.'

The butler shook his head. 'It is another blonde lady, not Miss Jansson. She says she is your mother, but I think maybe not?' He ended with a dubious look at Veronica.

Veronica jumped up. 'Sybil!' she gasped, as the blonde lady pushed her way into the yellow salon.

'Veronica! My darling child!' Sybil cried, and rushed to her, and clasped her in her arms. The tall stately blonde woman began to cry. 'Veronica, oh, poor poor darling! Diana wrote to me. I had to rush to you. Oh, my poor love! How your father would weep!' She touched the black silk sling on Veronica's arm, held her off from her to gaze at her anxiously, as tears streamed down her cheeks.

'Sybil—how did you—what—oh, my goodness—' Veronica was still gasping. Camilla had followed Sybil into the room. 'Sybil, darling, this is Pietro's sister, Camilla Cavalcanti, my dearest friend. She has been so good to me. Camilla, this is my stepmother, Sybil Murray, Mrs Murray.'

Camilla smiled her sweetest, but Sybil stared at her ominously. 'How do you do,' she muttered coldly to the young pretty girl, who stared at her in bewilderment. 'Do you mind? I wish

229

to speak to my daughter in private.'

Camilla blushed rosily, and backed from the room in confusion, her brown eyes hurt. Veronica could have struck her stepmother.

The door was closed softly. Veronica was alone with her stepmother. The woman was still in black, but it was a very attractive black velvet, thought Veronica. She had thrown back her black veil, and it framed her lovely blonde hair, set off her sparkling green eyes. Tears still streaked her cheeks.

'There's no time to argue,' said Sybil rapidly. 'Diana wrote to me, about those dreadful things happening to you. I knew—I knew it must be Pietro. I was against the marriage from the first. You can't tell what these foreigners will do! You must leave him. Leave him at once.'

'Leave him? Pietro?' Veronica gasped. She drew back, appalled. 'How could Diana... No, of course I won't leave him. He's my husband—he—'

'These things never happened to you when you were safe in my care!' Sybil told her authoritatively. 'I would never forgive myself if I didn't do my duty to Frank's only daughter! He entrusted you to me! I failed you. I let you marry and go off to Italy. I was so worried, my dear God, how I worried! When

230

I began receiving letters from Diana, I went frantic.'

'Where is Dr Heinrich?' Veronica interrupted, a cold chill going over her. That was the evil genius behind her stepmother, she thought. He must have sent her—or maybe he was here in Florence. The thought made her shiver.

Sybil stared at her, frowned impatiently. 'Don't change the subject! He's in New York, he has his practice. I see him occasionally—why?'

'Did he tell you to come to Italy, to persuade me to return to New York?'

'He didn't tell me! No. He is only my advisor. Veronica, don't dally. You must pack at once. I'll take you in my carriage. Leave the clothes, take your jewels only, we'll rush right off...'

'Where will you rush to?' the cold voice interrupted. Pietro had come silently into the yellow salon and was glaring at them.

Sybil whirled on him angrily, her tall figure commanding. 'I'm taking my daughter home! You have tried to kill her! You—you murderer! Yes, Diana Jansson wrote to me! She told me of the horrible *accidents* happening to Veronica! I won't believe you were not behind them!'

Veronica cried out, but Pietro's roar over-

231

whelmed her voice. 'How dare you! She is my wife! I would protect her with my life!'

'It doesn't look like it!' yelled Sybil, angrily, her face flushing. Camilla behind Pietro was looking wide-eyed and scared.

Veronica realized that Camilla had gone right for Pietro in his study, and brought him down.

'She is my wife! She is under my protection!' Pietro was yelling. 'Can I help it if the vendetta has started again? The Dossi...' He stopped abruptly, stared at Veronica. She stared back at him.

'What Vendetta? Who are the Dossi?' asked Veronica, but again her small voice was lost in the uproar.

'It is your vendetta! If she is killed, it is your fault! You can't protect her!' Sybil was screaming! All her composure was gone. She was red-faced, fiery-eyed, all tigress protecting her young.

Pietro yelled back at her, as though relieved to have the enemy at his throat, so he could fight something tangible. 'You—you couldn't protect your husband! Right in your home! At least I can protect Veronica!'

'What do you mean—my husband? He died of a strange illness...' Sybil began to calm down, staring at him frantically.

Pietro said more coldly, 'He died strangely,

yes. My wife is not returning to New York. It is more dangerous for her there than here.'

'More dangerous! She wasn't attacked with a knife there! She wasn't thrown from an old placid plug of a horse! No, strange things are going on! I must protect her! I would never forgive myself if Frank's daughter...' She turned impetuously to Veronica. 'Darling, darling come with me! At once. I will take care of you. This terrible man shan't touch you again...'

'Camilla, leave the room!' said Pietro.

Camilla was crying soundlessly. She shook her head, defying her brother for once, and went over to Veronica. 'Please, Veronica, don't listen,' she begged brokenly. 'Don't listen to her. Pietro loves you...we love you..'

Veronica put her arms around Camilla and hugged her. 'Sybil, please listen. Please listen to me,' she begged above the angry roars of her husband. 'Pietro—please! Sybil, I can't go back with you. My place is here. Please go. I won't discuss it further!'

Pietro didn't seem to hear her. He was raging at Sybil. 'My wife will never leave me! Get out! I won't let her go! She is my wife! I'll never let her go!'

Sybil glared at them. Pietro seemed to shoo her toward the door, out, into the hallway, stormily toward the front door. Veronica relaxed a little as she heard the angry voices fading into the outdoors, Pietro and Sybil angrily quarrelling right to the last.

Camilla was sobbing softly, as though grievously hurt. Veronica patted her shoulders. 'Calm yourself, Camilla, calm, you mustn't worry now. Please, darling, calm yourself...'

'Such wicked things,' Camilla cried. 'She said —such wicked—terrible—things—about *Pietro!*'

Pietro stormed back in, glaring at her accusingly as though she had invited Sybil there. Veronica glared back at him.

'So my wife has ideas about leaving me,' he began ominously.

'I do not! She came here. I didn't know she was even coming to Italy...'

'You must have invited her!'

'She came of her own will! Diana Jansson wrote to her...'

'What did she say? That I was beating you?' Pietro roared at her angrily. Veronica put her small hands over her ears.

'Please—stop it, don't fight!' Camilla begged them, beginning to cry all over again. 'Veronica, Pietro, I plead with you—don't fight—she isn't worth it! She makes trouble...'

The words seemed to have a calming effect on the angry troubled couple. The red flush began to fade from Pietro's face.

Veronica sighed deeply. 'She is right, Pietro. Sybil does make trouble. I'm sorry—I did not invite her. Please believe I did not invite Sybil here. I had no idea she was coming. She said she consulted with Dr Heinrich—I have an idea he urged her to come and order me home again.'

'She has no jurisdiction over you,' he said, coldly furious. 'You are my wife! You will do as I say!'

For some reason that stirred her anger again. She tried to suppress it. He was very dictatorial, she thought. Her mouth set, she stopped her pleading with him.

Pietro flung himself out of the house, was gone for several hours. He missed lunch, and caused caustic comment from Giorgio.

'What is going on?' asked the cousin. 'I understand your mother came from America, Veronica, and wishes you to return with her. What is happening?'

'She isn't Veronica's mother,' said Camilla, unexpectedly. 'She is her stepmother! She is a wicked woman!'

'She isn't wicked, Camilla,' said Veronica, wearily. 'She means well. And she is lonely in New York, she has written about that. She wanted me to stay with her a few months, and I refused. I feel guilty about that. She misses my father very much.'

'Then she should know better than to encourage you to leave your husband,' said Camilla passionately, her Botticelli face flushed pink. 'When a person loves, he—he understands!'

Giorgio eyes her curiously, his mouth curling a little in sarcasm. 'Now, what does our little cousin know...' he began.

'Please! No more,' said Veronica. 'How was the opera last Saturday, Giorgio? Tell us about it.'

'Scene by scene, I expect, little as you care about it,' he bantered goodnaturedly. 'Very well. In the first act, the lovely heroine stands weeping because her lover has left her—'

'Enough, Giorgio,' said Uncle Teodosio abruptly. He scarcely ever corrected his son. 'Let us have peace.'

Giorgio scowled, lost his humour and his appetite, and soon excused himself from the table. The lunch concluded in silence.

Veronica retired to the yellow salon where her work had been interrupted. This time she left the door to the hallway open so she could watch for Pietro's return.

It was late in the afternoon when she heard his voice, saw him stride past without a glance at her, and up the stairway. He looked dusty and tired, as though he had been riding for hours.

She leaned back in her chair, rubbed her arm thoughtfully. He looked so upset, he had been terribly angry at Sybil's suggestion that he was the cause of her accidents. But what if—not directly—but indirectly he was the cause of them? What if he had done something which had caused a vendetta to begin again? She knew what a vendetta was, and she had heard the name 'Dossi' whispered about.

Those many trips to Rome, sometimes with Giorgio—maybe they were not as innocent as they seemed. What if the business had to do with a family feud? Italians were passionate and wild, she thought. Pietro was capable of doing anything. He carried a knife and knew how to use it.

Was this why he felt so guilty? That he couldn't protect her? That he made her stay inside the villa and made Camilla stay in?

Or—was it something worse? She caught her breath at the horrible thought. Did he—was he connected with her father's death? Was the thought of the Murray money too much for him? Had he married her—only to kill her for the money?

She shuddered, and the bright yellow salon darkened before her eyes. All those accidents—

and the arsenic poisoning—they were not a coincidence. She had been hurt again and again, while Pietro had not suffered so much as a sprained finger. Any one of the attempts might have killed her.

'Mother of God, no!' she muttered. 'It can't be Pietro. I love him! I love him! He is my husband, and is good and kind—'

Frantically she began searching her mind for another solution. Dr Heinrich was not here in Florence, he was busy in his medical practice in New York. Yet the arsenic poisoning, the knifing, the pins in the horses' saddles had all occurred in Florence. So—who could have done it?

Not Pietro, no, not Pietro—

Who then? Giorgio?

Her mind fastened on the suave sarcastic cousin, the man who had never quite accepted her presence as mistress of his cousin's household. A cold man in many ways, a cool sophisticated man, with a knife, a desire to live like a prince. He had extravagant tastes.

And Andy thought Giorgio might have taken the gems from the safe in Florence. He had the combination. What if his craving for wealth was driving him on to madness?'

She shivered again and again, and finally stood up and paced the lovely yellow salon. She gazed at the lovely blue vases, empty now of their yellow roses. The roses were gone—and so were her illusions about the sunny happy life of Italy. There were dark passions under the surface. Camilla had told her stories, about the wars, the bloody battles between feuding families, the atrocities committed by one family on another. Poisoning, battles for power, fights in the streets of Florence until the cobblestones ran with red blood.

'No, I won't believe—I won't believe—' she was muttering as Camilla came down to her. The girl had dark shadows under her eyes, and she was still flushed with tears.

Dinner was intensely uncomfortably quiet. Pietro came down, but spoke only curtly. Giorgio was brooding and sullen. Uncle Teodosio was lost in his own thoughts. Camilla's voice was so husky from weeping that she seemed to dislike speaking. Veronica gave soft orders to the servants, ordered coffee at the table, and finally stood up in intense relief when they were finished.

She and Camilla spent the evening in the yellow salon. Camilla brought her embroidery, but seemed to have trouble seeing the work. Veronica looked at some books for ideas for designs, until her eyes felt dizzy with trying to read the old script.

They went up to bed early. Camilla kissed her goodnight, hugged her, was about to speak, and burst into tears instead. She went off sobbing to her own room.

Veronica went directly into her own room. She had not slept with Pietro, it seemed, for months. He never came to her room now. Her bed was turned down, her gown laid out. She undressed for bed, and then stood gazing a long time out the full-length French windows into the gardens below.

Moonlight lay like quivering flowers on the wilted winter garden, in small patches that flickered before her eyes. The hedges had begun to sprawl from the neat shapes of the summer. The fountain was silent, the dolphin lay alone.

She leaned her forehead against the cool glass. She was tired of thinking and worrying and wondering. She had no answers. She had only instinct to guide her. She had not wanted to go with Sybil today, she thought. She had felt instant anger and fury with Sybil for suggesting that Pietro was trying to murder her.

'I don't believe that,' she murmured aloud. 'I just don't believe that! He is kind and good. Yes, he has a fierce temper but he has never struck me, or been cruel to me. Surely, surely that is a sign—'

She thought for a long time. She saw lights flickering on the balcony from Pietro's room. Presently they were dimmed, went out. Pietro had blown out his candles and gone to bed.

She was a little cold from standing so long. She made a resolution and acted on it before thought and reason could stop and stifle her instinct. She did trust him. She trusted him, she loved him. That was all that mattered to her.

She picked up her robe from the bed, and flung it around her shoulders. She went steadily over to the closed door that separated their bedrooms and tapped lightly.

She heard nothing. She opened the door and walked into his bedroom. It was silent, dark, lit only by the moonlight coming through his French windows.

'Pietro?' she murmured, trying to see him, peering forward into the darkness.

'Si?' he answered from the big bed.

She walked slowly across the carpets. It seemed a long walk, yet she arrived before her words were ready. He sat up in bed.

'Pietro—please—please forgive me for doubting you,' she burst out. 'I do trust you. I love you.'

There was a moment of silence, as though he had been struck dumb. 'Veronica,' he said, softly.

She sat down on the bedside. She reached blindly for his hand, found the big warm hand stretched out to hers. She clasped it as though it might be an anchor to hold her fast. 'I love you,' she repeated.

He gave a big sigh that was half a sob. 'Veronica—cara—I love you so much—Veronica—' he drew her down on the bed, flung the robe off, drew her under the covers with him, into the warmth of his arms.

Oh, this was where she wanted to be. She snuggled down happily into his possessive arms, felt his kisses on her cheeks, her lips, her closed eyes, over her throat and arms. He muttered caresses with the caresses of his mouth and hands. Yet he was so gentle, so careful—

She felt once again the wonderful ecstasy of his embrace. Only this time he said again and again, in English and in Italian, 'I love you, I love, I love you—'

Her hands caressed his head as he held her tightly. Her small hands went over his head and shoulders and back, learning him all over again, hungry after the long denial. It was a long time before they slept.

They lay in bed long the next morning, talking sleepily, saying the frank words they had not said before. She told him about the theft of the Contessa's gems from the safe in Florence.

'And you did not tell me?' he reproached, but he did not take his arms from around her.

'Oh, Pietro, I'm sorry. But I feared—I was afraid that perhaps Giorgio had taken them. I don't know what to think. I can't repay the Contessa yet, not until I'm twenty-one. And this might ruin the firm. What shall we do?'

'We will decide later,' he said, after a pause. 'We must think and I shall try to discover who did the theft. There are other suspects than Giorgio, you know.'

She knew he meant Andy Kelly, but she did not respond. She did not want to spoil the wonderful night.

It was almost noon when she left the warm nest of his bed, and put on her robe again. She pushed open the door to her room which she had closed after coming into Pietro's. Then she gasped, and cried out.

Pietro jumped out of bed and was in her room as soon as she had stepped inside. Together they stared at the chaos. The French windows were wide open, and a strong winter wind blew the curtains and drapes aside. Muddy footprints led from the balcony around the blue and white rug, around and around the room. Her dresser drawers were yanked open, powder spilled, boxes opened. Jewellery dripped from some formerly-locked cases on the tall chest.

'My God,' Veronica cried. 'Pietro...' She turned and held tightly to him. 'If I hadn't gone to your room last night...'

'You would have been here—in bed,' he muttered. His arms closed hard, fiercely around her. 'Mother of God...'

'But how did anyone get here. The balcony—no one could climb up.'

She drew back and stared up into his face. He stared down at her. There was only one way to the balcony—through their suite of rooms. Someone had been inside the Villa d'Oro last night. Someone? a stranger? Or someone familiar to them, who would rob and murder?

CHAPTER 15

Pietro sent for Camilla, Maria, the servants. They ran around frantically, trying to find the intruder, but of course he had disappeared hours before. Then Camilla, Maria, and Veronica settled down to figure out what was missing.

Pietro came back from touring the grounds, and came into her bedroom. 'Have you discovered what has been stolen?' he asked, his face drawn and anxious.

'Two strands of pearls,' said Veronica, quietly. 'One set of rubies, the ones my father left to me. I think those are the only valuable jewels. The man must have tried the locks on the small chests, but was unable to pry them open. Some costume jewellery is gone, but there was no value there.'

'Who would do such a thing?' cried Maria, in Italian.

'Who was able to get into the villa?' asked Camilla, her brown eyes so worried that Veronica leaned over and kissed her.

No one could solve it. Veronica dismissed the servants, washed and dressed. It was mid-afternoon, and she was hungry. She and Pietro went down to join Camilla in a very late lunch in the dining room.

Giorgio and Teodosio returned later from a long ride, and were amazed at the news. They had seen and heard no one strange, nothing had happened. Giorgio said he had been up early and had seen no one but the servants working around.

They discussed the situation over their coffee in the yellow salon. Giorgio said he would arm the guards, post them on sentry duty at night, supervise them himself. He had some wild plans until Pietro calmed him down.

'Well, at least I have some nice designs worked out for you,' said Giorgio. He got up, went over to the desk, opened a drawer and drew out some sketches.

'Designs?' asked Veronica, stunned as he handed her the sketches. She began to look them over. She felt cold as she saw his intention.

'For the Contessa Guilia d'Antoniazzo. You see, I will make the tiara small and modest, with a single blazing ruby in the centre of some widely-spaced baroque pearls. Matching this will be the pendant, another large ruby hanging in an oval of more baroque pearls.'

'But—Giorgio—the pearls and rubies of the Contessa have been stolen,' said Pietro.

Camilla gasped, and set down her cup and saucer with a small clatter. Her face went white. 'They were in Veronica's room?' she whispered.

'No, from the safe. They were stolen from the safe,' said Veronica. 'Oh, Pietro, we cannot hide the theft forever! Whatever shall we do?' After the joy of last night, her descent to despair had been sudden and shocking. Someone hated them, she thought. Someone hated them enough to murder her, to ruin them financially, to steal in at night. She shuddered violently.

'Calm yourself, Veronica.' Pietro placed his hand on her shoulder as he stood near her chair. 'Calm yourself. We shall manage this—'

'Stolen? They can't be stolen,' Giorgio interrupted. 'I saw them—when were they stolen?'

'Weeks ago,' said Pietro.

Giorgio stared at his cousin, his black eyes narrowed, his face alert. 'No, that cannot be,' he said, flatly. 'They are in the safe. I will show you.' He stood up, went over to a large painting on the wall of the yellow salon.

Veronica forgot her despair, forgot her troubles, watched with wide wondering eyes as he drew the painting out from the wall with one side swinging loose. Behind it was a flat wall-safe, a combination. Giorgio flipped the dial around with practised ease. Easily, very easily, he opened the large safe, and reached into it. He drew out the velvet-wrapped packets of jewels.

Pietro strode over to Giorgio, grabbed a packet, opened it onto a table. The gems spilled their ruby radiance in the darkened room, like red sunlight. He laughed aloud in relief. 'There they are! They are here, Veronica! They are not lost. Thank God. Thank God!'

After the moments of relief, Veronica began to chill again. She stared at the gems the men spilled out on the table. Giorgio thrust them back and forth with his large fingers, his face lighted now, eager, proud. 'Aren't they beautiful?' he exclaimed. 'Aren't they lovely? See the designs I made, Veronica. What do you think?'

Almost blindly, she gazed down at the designs, looked from one sketch to another. They were not just good, they were brilliant. He was a true artist, she thought. 'They are very very good, Giorgio,' she said, at last, her voice intensely quiet. 'They are excellent. I have never seen such lovely designs. The Contessa would be immensely pleased with them. They will suit her style of beauty and enhance it.'

At her praise, Giorgio's face lit up, he beamed like a child. Pietro grinned all over, excitedly, came to her, took the sketches and glanced over them. 'They are good, good,' he said, in Italian, his hands shaking. 'Oh, what a relief. The gems are here, and the Contessa's designs are made—a relief, eh, Veronica?' He touched her cheek affectionately. 'My little one, you are cold,' he added, anxiously. His warm palm stroked over her cheek and neck.

248

Camilla asked the question Veronica wanted to ask. 'But why did you take the gems from the safe in Florence, without telling anyone, Giorgio?' she asked, reproachfully. 'You would know they would worry.'

He shrugged. 'I didn't think they would miss them. They have so much to work on, they didn't have time to work on these. I thought if I could design something good, I would return the gems quietly, and no one the wiser.'

Pietro added his reproach, but Giorgio only shrugged and laughed. He did not seem to think he had done anything wrong. Veronica wondered again, more seriously than ever. Was Giorgio like Pietro, an honest man, or did he think nothing of stealing gems? She went further. If Giorgio had stolen once, would he steal again? Had he decided to return the Contessa's gems, so the Murray business would not fail, but had taken Veronica's own jewels to sell for his own purposes?

She did not know Giorgio. He could act well, he could deceive and conceal his true motives. She did not know what he was truly like inside. She did not know if he might be capable of theft—and murder. How much would a gentleman, poor for years, do to obtain money and wealth again? Plenty, she thought. A great deal.

'Well, do you like the designs?' Giorgio was asking her eagerly. He seemed truly intent on her answer.

'I like them very much,' she said, rousing herself from despair. 'They are extremely good, Giorgio. You are a born artist. I wish—' She hesitated, then plunged. 'I wish you would show these to Andy Kelly, explain them, go ahead on the designing of the Contessa's gems. Then, perhaps, you might go on with designing for us. Pietro will work out the salary for you. You could work just when you wished, but you know we have a great many commissions to do. We need another skilled designer.'

Giorgio stared at her, then broke into a wide grin. 'Agreed!' he said, with satisfaction. 'If you think I can do it...'

'You can do it, you can,' said Pietro firmly. He seemed both surprised and intensely relieved. 'Whatever Giorgio sets out to do, he does!'

Uncle Teodosio came into the room, his face shadowed, his silvery hair gleaming in the candlelit salon. 'So what has Giorgio done now?' he asked mildly.

He was told, explained to, shown the designs. He nodded, thoughtfully, took less interest than Veronica would have expected. He did not seem upset at the idea of his son going into trade, she thought, wryly. Maybe when it was his own son, anything was respectable.

With his usual gentlemanly courtesy, he waited till their excitement had calmed, the subject temporarily exhausted, before bringing up his own activities.

'I have been questioning the servants and the grooms,' he said, in his courtly manner. 'I think I have discovered something. With the permission of my cousin's wife, I wish to call Maria.'

'Maria! Oh, she hasn't—she hasn't—' Camilla began brokenly.

He reassured her with a glance and a nod. 'I think she has discovered something for us,' he said. Giorgio dashed out, and returned with the red-faced maid. She had been waiting outside, twisting her hands in her apron.

'Tell them, Maria. Just as you told me,' Uncle Teodosio told her gently.

She looked at them anxiously, finally turned to Veronica. 'Madonna, I watched. I thought about the poison. And the Dossi family, the vendetta. Everybody I watch. And the new gardener is always hanging around the kitchen in the morning whenever I am fixing your coffee. He says he wants some coffee. I tell him to go, but he comes back next morning. That one, he always hangs around and listens, with his muddy shoes tracking up the floor.'

'Muddy shoes!' Veronica looked from Maria to Pietro. He was leaning forward, staring at the maid.

'You said—the Dossi family,' he urged.

'Yes, sir. He is new about here, but I asked my cousins in Florence. They said the Dossi are back, sir. They have been seen. Now this one, I don't know if he is one of them, he doesn't have the look of a Dossi, but he was hanging around, and he could have put poison in the madonna's coffee,' said Maria, nodding firmly, her face bright red with the effort at expressing herself.

Giorgio had already disappeared, back to the servants' quarters. He returned presently. 'The man is gone,' he said shortly. 'The gardener disappeared this morning. No one has seen him since about ten o'clock.'

The men and Camilla broke out into an excited chatter. Veronica waited patiently, and finally was able to ask her question. 'Who are the Dossi? Why are they important?'

Pietro came over to her and sat down beside her, taking her hand. He looked intensely relieved. 'They are the family which my family banned from Florence many years ago,' he said. 'The vendetta had gone on a long time. It would take a long time to tell of their insults, their injuries. They murdered an uncle of my father, they attempted murder on my father and uncle. Finally my father banished them. They have not dared to return until now.'

'This explains the attacks on Veronica and Pietro,' said Giorgio, with authority. 'The Dossi have returned! Well, we shall banish them, and they shall stay banished this time! If they stay, it will be murder!' He looked fierce.

Veronica thought of her father, dying in New York, of the attack on shipboard. No, this was not the whole answer, she thought, as the men spoke of the Dossi, of finding them, of sending them away. Maria beamed, the heroine of the occasion, full of pride at solving the mystery.

'The muddy footprints in the bedroom this morning,' said Camilla. 'That must have been the gardener, hired by the Dossi. And he stole Veronica's jewels!'

'Yes, those shall be returned,' said Pietro. 'We shall locate them. I shall inform the Marchese at once, the authorities in Florence...'

'This explains everything,' said Giorgio.

Camilla looked at Veronica, and caught the gaze of her sister-in-law. The two women gazed at each other. Each knew the thought in the mind of the other. No, it did not explain everything.

Maria was promised a lavish reward, and

253

went away to chatter her story in the kitchens and servants' quarters. Giorgio left to muster the guard and admonish them about the peril. Teodosio left to take a nap, he was exhausted. Pietro and Veronica discussed the Contessa's gems, and then he went to the upstairs study to work, leaving the yellow salon to her.

'I know you prefer this room for working,' he said, with a smile. 'Eh, it will be good to have Giorgio helping us, yes?'

'Yes, that will be very good,' she said, soberly. The memory returned anew, of Giorgio's dark face as he exclaimed against the Dossi, of his cheerful lack of concern when discovered in a theft of removing the gems from the safe in Florence. Giorgio, the dark uncertain one, the jealous one, the man who had been rich and now was poor. The man who had been against the marriage of Veronica and Pietro, then suddenly indifferent. The man who had been on shipboard, who had worn a black cloak on shipboard, like the person who had attacked Veronica, almost pushing her into the ocean.

Giorgio, the trusted cousin of Veronica's husband. The man who loved dramatics, to act and play the clown, the man who liked to manoeuvre people, to manipulate lives, to encourage Veronica to stay with Pietro. Giorgio, who had admitted taking the jewels of the

254

Contessa. Giorgio, the man who carried a knife and knew how to use it.

No, thought Veronica, staring sightlessly at the designs, everything was not explained. Not at all. She remembered that Giorgio had been in New York for the months preceding her father's death of poisoning.

CHAPTER 16

The next few days passed in a whirl of activity. Pietro was constantly making plans, meeting the Marchese, going down to Florence to receive reports about the Dossi's activities. Giorgio was full of importance about his part in the discovery, of his new work. Teodosio slept placidly in his favourite chair, he had done his part to uncover the plot.

Only Camilla and Veronica remained worried. They talked once, briefly, but Veronica could not bring herself to voice her suspicions of Giorgio.

One morning in mid-February, as rain beat down on the long French windows, Maria brought Veronica a note in the yellow salon where she was working.

'For you, madonna. The messenger has gone. He said it was extremely important.' She looked puzzled and frightened.

'Thank you, Maria. You may go.' Veronica took the note, looked at the writing. It was Diana's she thought. Probably an invitation to something.

The maid curtsied and withdrew. Veronica broke open the envelope and stared at the brief lines within. They were hastily written, lines streaming up and down the page, as though Diana had been interrupted, excited, upset.

'Darling Veronica. I have discovered the facts. You must come to Florence at once, to-day. Don't trust anyone! Don't tell Pietro, for he would not believe—families stick together— but your life is more important. Come at once! I can explain everything now! The strange events fit together, believe me. I can trust nothing to a note. Your life is in grave danger. Come at once! Your loving Diana.'

Veronica's hands began to shake. She set down the note, and stared at it. Diana had been talking to people in Florence, she had a strong charming way of making friends, finding out what she wanted to know. She would discover if anyone could and she had managed to do so.

It must be Giorgio. That was what Diana was afraid to say in the note. It had to be Giorgio.

Pietro would never believe it. She must go to Florence, get the facts from Diana, and tell Giorgio in such a firm way that they knew the truth—

She carried the note with her, and went out into the hall. Maria stood there, twisting her hands anxiously, her face troubled.

'Maria, tell the groom I wish to ride this morning. I want Pietro's horse,' she said, very firmly. 'I will be ready in ten minutes.'

'But—madonna!' the girl wailed. 'The signore...he will not permit...not to ride alone...'

'Do as I say,' said Veronica, curtly, and ran up the stairs.

She changed to a servicable dark blue habit that could withstand the rain better than her blue velvet. She crammed her blonde hair under a full veil, and fastened it down tightly. She hesitated a moment, then took a fine ruby ring from her jewel box. Diana would appreciate a reward. She put the ring on her finger, so it would look natural for her to remove it and give it to Diana.

She ran down the stairs again, her riding crop under her arm. Again she hesitated, then she went into the yellow salon. In the drawer was a small but sharp knife, sheathed. She took it, and thrust the sheath and knife into the deep pocket of her riding skirt.

257

The horse was waiting at the door, the tall black stallion that was Pietro's favourite. The groom waited with it, and another horse, ready to ride with her.

'Thank you,' she said curtly. 'I shall not need you today. Go.' She accepted his lift into the saddle, and stared down at him firmly.

He looked from her face to Maria's as the maid waited at the huge doors. 'But madonna, I must ride with you. Orders...the duke has said...'

'No!' said Veronica, and flung away, pulling the huge horse as though she knew just what she was doing. The horse was straining eagerly to run. He was more horse than she had ever tried to handle, but she knew her placid old favourite would never stand the ride to Florence.

She glanced back once. The groom had not dared to follow her. He stood beside the tall brown horse, watching her gloomily, and chatting to Maria. No, he would not follow her.

She let the stallion break into a run as they came out into the lane. He was fresh and eager, not ridden for several days. He pranced, and she caught her breath, then held him in firmly. She must not let him get away from her. There was no groom here to help her, no Pietro to rescue her.

She turned him into the lane toward the road that led up from Florence to Fiesole. Once into the road, on the wet slippery road with the rain pouring down, the stallion settled into a good stride. She hunched her shoulders against the downpour, the veil protecting her hair somewhat, and let her face be washed by the cool gusty wind. Her mind was in a daze. What was the truth? What would be Pietro's reaction? Would he hate her forever? Would he send her away?

She caught herself from the desolate thoughts that plagued her. She would handle that later, she thought. Pietro loved her, she loved him. At least she believed that was so. Pietro had come to love her, he had told her so, his arms and embraces had proved it. He was so tender, so gentle, so loving. Even when he learned the truth about Giorgio, he would not hate her. Would he? She bit her lips till they stung. One thing at a time, she reminded herself. Diana's story must come first.

There was little traffic on the road that gloomy, rainy day. A donkey cart passed her, moving slowly uphill. She heard the driver shout a greeting moments later. Curious, when she heard the shouted reply, she turned around in the saddle.

She froze. A man in a black cloak was following her! A man in black, on a tall brown horse —Giorgio!

She recognized him partly by his build, partly by his way of riding, leaning forward slightly, one arm swinging loose.

'Oh, God,' she moaned, and urged her horse on a little faster. It was dangerous to go too fast on the wet winding road. She set her face forward, not daring to turn back again. Giorgio was following her, and chill fear invaded her, not to leave for a long time. Pietro was somewhere in Florence, she had no knowledge of where he was. The groom would not follow her. There was no one to help her—except Diana.

The road downward seemed endless, yet abruptly it came to an end, and the road was level in Florence. She gave the stallion free rein, and galloped recklessly through the narrow streets. She glanced back once—Giorgio was galloping also, always just at an even distance behind her. Her hands were cold, her feet were cold. The tall horse was almost more than she could handle. He kept shaking his head, impatient at the bit, and she was afraid he would take fright at something and go madly through the streets.

Perhaps he was just following out of curiosity. He made no attempt to catch up with her.

Triumph began to flood through her. She would reach Diana's, and Giorgio could not know Diana had a precious message for her.

A man shouted a curse at her, as his horse sheered against hers. She pulled down the stallion and made her way more sedately into the narrow streets nearer to Diana's apartment. One more turn, another. She turned into the street in front of Diana's apartment. There were horse troughs, places to fasten her horse near Diana's—she glanced back. Giorgio was not in sight.

But men moved in from the street in front of her. Dark-faced—who were they? She recognized a face, and began to shake. The man who had attacked her after the concert!

The man with the knife! He was near her. He was grinning. She dashed past him unexpectedly, the black stallion lashing out with his hoofs. The man fell back, then ran after her, shouting.

'The woman! The woman!' he was yelling. Another man came from behind a building. A shopkeeper peered out from a door, then ducked inside again.

She was near the apartment. She reined up abruptly, the stallion reared, then settled down, tired from his long ride. She slid down and ran! She left the stallion untied, loose in the street, her own life was more precious.

She ran and ran, made it to the door of the apartment building. The street door was un-locked—she got in—to the elevator—got the elevator—and it began its slow ride upward. Men were dashing up the stairs, she could see them at the levels.

The elevator was slightly faster than the men, and the apartment was on the sixth floor. Veronica began to scream aloud as she neared the sixth flight. 'Diana! Diana! Help! Men are following me! Diana—Diana—'

As the elevator door opened, she saw Diana's door opening. She ran for it. The men were climbing from the fifth floor.

Veronica got inside Diana's door. Diana, tall, blonde, was staring at her. Veronica tried to get the door closed against the men. 'Help me—those men—following—' she panted.

Diana struck her in the face, driving her back into the room. Stunned and shocked, Veronica fell back onto a couch. She glared in fury and amazement as Diana held the door open for the men.

'Come in. All that commotion,' she said. 'You make too much noise. People will hear you!'

The men shrugged sullenly, and came in. They stood staring at Veronica, curiously, not touching her.

'Well, dear Veronica, you fell into our little trap!' It was Sybil's voice. She had approached the girl soundlessly from one of the bedrooms. Veronica got up, whirled around, her eyes going wide. 'Good work, Diana. After all our failures, we shall at last succeed!'

'All I want is the money,' said Diana sullenly, as Veronica looked at her, silently accusing.

'Get on with it.' Sybil motioned to the men. One came forward, the knife in his hand looking long and menacing. His dark evil face shone at the girl, but he seemed to hesitate.

She sat down, and folded her hands in her lap. Her intense calm seemed to puzzle them. 'Wait,' said Veronica. 'First, I want the explanation Diana promised me. Who are these men?'

It threw them off for a moment. Sybil shook her head, as though dazed. 'Oh, what does that matter? They are the Dossi, they have a vendetta with your husband's family. Glad to kill for pay. But the stupid ones, they were always distracted by the jewels. They would have killed you at the Pergola, if Carlo there hadn't stopped to snatch your pearls! The damn fool.'

Carlo snarled, his knife drooping a little. The three other men growled at him, asking a question in Italian. 'Why are you waiting, mad one? Get it over. They will come.'

Veronica stared intently at Sybil. She didn't understand Italian. She moved her hand slightly, imperiously, at Carlo. 'Wait,' she said in Italian. 'I want to hear the explanation first.' She switched to English rapidly, and addressed Sybil as the surprised man stared at her. 'Tell me about my father. Did you kill him, or was it Doctor Heinrich?'

Diana cried out. 'Oh, get it over! I hate the waiting! Get it over!'

'Was it Doctor Heinrich?' Veronica asked Sybil calmly. 'I suspected him. I didn't think you had the brains to figure out arsenic poisoning.'

'What are you saying?' cried Sybil, her blonde face flushing. 'It was my plan, always my plan! Your damn fool father wouldn't give me any money! I decided to take it all! Only he left it to you! Then I had to kill you next!'

'So you poisoned my father with arsenic, and killed him. Then on shipboard—was that a Dossi man?'

'That was me,' said Diana, smiling a little with some amusement. Her greenish-grey eyes sparkled at the memory. 'Oh, you were so easy to fool! It was a pity! My act was wasted.'

'Not wasted,' said Veronica, conversationally. Her hands were ice cold. She wondered if she did snatch out her knife if her hands were too cold to use it. 'I wondered why you had changed so much from convent days. You never liked me then...'

'I hated you! I always hated you!' said Diana, the smile gone, her face twisting into ugliness. 'My money was gone, lost, and you were always *treating*. God, I hated you, your condescension, your gentle meekness, and the way the nuns fawned over you and your damn money! Well, I'll have money now! Sybil promised me...'

'And my morning coffee,' said Veronica, very calmly. Diana's rage was beginning to stir up the men again. Carlo was approaching her slowly, his big muddy feet quiet on the expensive rug. 'Was that your work, Sybil? How did you manage that?'

'Diana hired a man to do your gardening. The big fool bungled it. He was not subtle enough. Then he ran off with your jewels. I made him give me the jewels—then Carlo here killed him. He was a fool,' added Sybil, again, callously.

'Well, that helps explain things,' said Veronica, calmly. In Italian, 'No, Carlo, not yet. Not yet. I want to hear more.' In English,

'Now, tell me how you thought to get hold of the Murray business. It would have gone to Pietro...'

'Enough talking!' cried Sybil, alarmed. 'I hear someone. Kill her, Carlo—' She gestured toward Veronica elaborately, made a motion of slitting her own throat. 'Kill! Kill!'

In a moment the door was slamming inward, and Pietro, Giorgio and several men raged into the room. Veronica jumped up, and leaped in an unlady-like haste over the back of the chair, and behind it, near her stepmother who gaped at the intrusion.

The Dossi turned to meet the invasion. Diana screamed. Giorgio swiped with his knife, his dark face red with rage, and caught a Dossi man with it. The man, with dark red blood covering his stomach, fell to the floor, holding himself, groaning.

Pietro was fighting with Carlo, the tall mean one. Veronica held her breath. Teodosio was having a bad time with another one, and one of the servants—the groom, Veronica recognized him—came to his rescue, the two men fighting the Dossi man. Diana interfered, clawing, a knife in her long white hand, her face distorted with rage.

Giorgio turned to face Diana, rather unsure of himself now, his chivalry not wanting to soil

266

itself by knifing a lady. She thrust at him, he held her off with his long arm, his knife circling uneasily at her.

Pietro turned his head anxiously to Veronica. In that moment, someone struck him from behind, and Carlo knocked him down flat. Pietro's head struck the corner of a table, and he subsided, his face going blank.

The sight made a tigress of Veronica. She leaped at Sybil, her knife in her hands. In a moment, she had caught the older, taller woman by the hair, and ripped at it. Viciously, she held the woman down, her hand tight in the loose blonde hair. She held her over the end of the couch, gazing down into the green eyes, the green eyes that had been so calm and full of hate. Now they were startled, scared— now frightened and wild—

'Dossi!' Veronica screamed. She held her knife pointed at the pulse of her stepmother's throat. 'Dossi! Let them alone. Or I will kill this one! Dossi! Off them!' she screamed in Italian. 'Sybil—' she added then in English. 'Call them off—or you die! You die!'

The knife pricked at the long white throat, and blood met the point. Sybil moaned, gutturally. 'Don't—don't—'

'Call them off! Call them off!' Veronica screamed. The knife bit more deeply. More blood spurted. She felt wild and primitive. Her man was hurt. She would kill!

Sybil yelled then. 'No, no, no! Stop! Dossi, stop! Let them go! Let them go!'

She got the message known, with some translation from Veronica. The Dossi men got up reluctantly. Veronica stared darkly, not letting go her stepmother's hair, the knife at her throat. Her gaze fell on her husband's face, so blank, so quiet.

Diana was sobbing, crouching on the floor. Giorgio had her knife, and the long white arm had a streak of blood on it.

'Giorgio, see to Pietro,' said Veronica. 'If he is hurt, this one dies.'

'Si, Veronica,' said Giorgio, quietly. He went over to Pietro, knelt, wiped the white face. He took some wine from a bottle on the table, splashed it, held it to Pietro's mouth. Pietro sputtered, opened his eyes, dazed, looking about.

There was a long pause in the room. The groom stood at the door, knife at the ready. Another servant helped Teodosio to his feet. The Dossi crouched together, anxiously, their eyes on Pietro, veering to Sybil, still at Veronica's mercy.

Pietro got to his feet, with Giorgio's help. He stared at the people in the room, longest at his wife, with knife held in ready hand at her step-mother's throat. His gaze was thoughtful.

Veronica spoke, the words coming with difficulty. Her throat felt raw from screaming. 'Sybil poisoned my father. She paid Diana to try to kill me. She hired the Dossi to kill both of us.'

'Ah, ah,' muttered Giorgio, nodding. 'As I thought.'

Pietro turned to the Dossi men. 'I banish you,' he said, so gently they had to lean forward to hear his words. His dark eyes glittered. 'I banish you as my father did, only farther. You will go, you will leave Italy. Never to return. Not you or your family or your cousins, or your grandchildren will ever return to Italy. I banish you. The Marchese and all authorities will be informed. If you return, I shall murder you all. Go.'

They did not wait. They backed to the door, fairly ran down the stairs, their feet tromping heavily in their haste. Pietro turned to Diana.

'And you. Leave Italy, or you too will be murdered,' he said, in English. 'If you ever touch me or my wife or our family or anyone dear to us, you shall be murdered. Do you understand?'

His accent was thick, but she understood. The blonde head nodded, bent down.

'And you,' he said to Sybil. 'You are the worst. You are a murderess. You killed to get money. You killed your own husband. Murderess, you will leave. You will return to the house you stole, to the money you covered with your blood and the blood of your husband. Never see us again. Never write, never speak. Or you will lose everything. Do you understand?'

She glared at him, as Veronica let her up slowly. The point of the knife was covered with blood, and a trickle of blood ran down her white throat. 'I understand,' she said, very bitterly.

'Then we go. Come, Veronica,' he said. She went over to him, and his arm went around her closely. They left together, and were followed by Giorgio, Teodosio, and last the two servants.

Several horses and a carriage waited at the apartment entrance. The groom held the black stallion who was still trembling with nervousness. 'I'll ride that one back. The carriage for you,' said Giorgio. 'I always suspected the Dossi,' he said.

Veronica stopped him, a hand on his arm. 'Thank you, Giorgio,' she said, in Italian. 'I—suspected you. Please forgive me. I will never doubt you again.'

'Eh!' he said, embarrassed, grinning a little. 'Well, we have been strange to you, eh? But now, you are a Cavalcanti, in truth, eh? We have fought side by side.'

He patted her arm, and went over to the black stallion, mounted him. Pietro helped Veronica into the carriage.

'Don't scold me, Pietro,' she begged faintly. 'I know I was wrong to come at Diana's note but I was so mixed up...'

'We will not need to speak about it again,' he said, firmly. 'Only, you must learn to obey your husband, Veronica. When will you ever learn?'

'I am learning,' she said, cuddling thankfully into his warm arms, as the horses started out.

He did not keep his word. He scolded her all the way back to the villa, but she did not mind. He was holding her tightly, his hand stroking her blonde hair, her cheeks, her throat. He was talking in loving tones even as he reproached her for not trusting them, for going off without the groom, for going to Florence alone, for everything he could think of.

But the danger was over, she thought. She was safe, from the dark nightmare, the fears, the cold horror of the unknown killer. That was over. The truth was known, in the open, where they could fight. Where they could win, together.

CHAPTER 17

Veronica lay on the lounge chair, her eyes closed, luxuriating in the April sunshine that spread like a healing balm over her and the greening garden. The long difficult strange winter was over, her first winter in Florence.

Now she felt truly at home. This was her home her haven, her sanctuary, her domain. The servants had begun to come to her for orders instead of Camilla. Timidly at first, then with more confidence, she had begun to run the household as the Duchess of Isola d'Oro should run it. Pietro's wife, his loved and loving wife, she thought, and smiled vaguely, opening her eyes.

Yesterday had been a full tiring exciting day. Andy Kelly and Giorgio had returned from their trip to America, full of reports, gossip, news, orders, the latest from America. The New York shop was as busy as the Florence shop with the orders, Murray's was more popular than ever. Andy would be returning again to America in two more months, then back again.

A figure bent over her, lips gently touched her cheek. She opened her eyes again drowsily, and smiled up at Pietro.

'Darling, you are all right? Not ill?' he asked, anxiously. 'Was yesterday too much for you? You seem so weary.'

She sat up with an effort. She had not told him yet, the moment had not been right. But soon she would tell him.

'I'm fine, caro. Is it time for Andy to arrive?'

Pietro grimaced. 'Yes. I think he is going to live with us,' he sighed. 'Why did I ever agree for him to court Camilla?'

'Because I begged you and so did Camilla,' replied Veronica, a twinkle in her eyes. 'Oh—they are coming now.' She twisted around to watch as Giorgio, Andy and Camilla came down the stone steps into the gardens.

Camilla was radiant, so lovely one blinked to see her. She seemed to have changed from a girl to a woman overnight, thought Veronica fondly. Her face shone, her dark eyes sparkled, there was a sweetness and loveliness about her that made one look again and again at her. Certainly Andy was doing so. He could scarcely take his eyes from her as she moved quickly in her pink gown across the green lawns.

'So—here we are again,' said Giorgio, exuberantly, flinging himself down on one of the chairs as soon as Camilla was seated. 'This business—it is exhausting. I think I'll give it up!'

They all laughed at him. He was a changed man, now that he was one of the designers, working full-time, throwing himself into work as he had previously disdained it. He had now an outlet for the frustrated artistic instincts that had embittered him in his earlier years. He was earning his own money, could spend it as he pleased. He had courted five girls in New York, said Andy, and Giorgio had only laughed at the charge.

'You have been to the shop?' Veronica asked Andy.

He reluctantly looked away from Camilla for a moment. 'Yes. The new man, Paolo, is doing quite well. He's young, but he has the artistic touch. I turned over another job to him, and gave him a raise, as you suggested.'

They talked business for a few minutes, but Andy and Giorgio plainly didn't have their minds on work, for differing reasons. It was late afternoon, warm in the sunlight, and Giorgio kept yawning. Andy kept gazing at Camilla, from whom he had been separated for two months.

'Did you—did you see Sybil in New York?' Veronica finally asked Andy.

The men all scowled, stared at each other, then at the ground. Pietro finally answered.

'Giorgio said she is going to be married to Dr Heinrich. She has closed the Murray house, and plans to sell it. The servants were all dismissed.'

'Oh—oh, no!' Veronica gasped, thinking of Jennie, the butler, all the faithful—

'Father took care of them,' Andy said quickly, reassuringly. 'We have your devoted Jennie, and love her. Whenever you come back to New York, you must stay with us and let her spoil you again.'

'Oh, dear Jennie! I will write at once to Mr Kelly and thank him. He is so thoughtful and kind. But Sybil—is she staying—'

Pietro again answered Veronica. 'She has left New York. I think gossip has trickled out about her and the doctor, and your father's mysterious death. She was made to feel quite unwelcome. Evidently they are moving out West somewhere. That episode is ended, Veronica. You must forget it,' he added sternly.

She nodded. The doctor had said the same thing. She had had nightmares for a while, but Pietro had slept with her, soothed her, comforted her with his words and his kisses. The nightmares were fading, so were the vivid memories of the horrible events.

Giorgio yawned again and again.

'Dear Giorgio,' said Veronica, rather ironically. 'We are keeping you awake with our chatter! Do go to your room and have some sleep!'

They all laughed as he rose promptly, kissed her hand pompously, and took formal leave of them. He fairly ran up the steps to the house, disappearing inside.

'He did work like a trooper in New York,' said Andy. They had become good friends on the trip, that was obvious. 'When he decides to do anything, he really does it!'

'That was always true of Giorgio,' said Pietro.

Veronica thought it was also true of her husband. Perhaps it was a trait of the Cavalcanti! As soon as the truth was known about the mysterious events, Pietro had moved into action. He had rehired Maddalena. He had called the servants together, and told them the whole dramatic story, formally apologized to Maddalena and to her entire family, paid her double wages for the time she had been gone. He had gone to the Marchese, told him the story, sent word out that the Dossi were banished.

All Florence had talked of nothing else for a week, until something else had happened, an opera star eloping with a married man, and they had something else to discuss over their coffee.

Now their own story had faded into history, thought Veronica. She was glad of it!

Andy was looking at Camilla longingly. Veronica took pity on them.

'Camilla, show Andy the flowers along the hedge, how pretty they are,' she said. 'And the new rose garden near the fountain.'

They jumped up, beaming, and were off hand-in-hand before Pietro could open his mouth. He frowned after them.

'They won't be out of sight, besides he can be trusted, Pietro,' said Veronica. Her hand reached out for his big one and clasped it. 'And I wanted to be alone with you for once! We are always in a crowd these days!'

He clasped her small hand tightly, and then lifted it to his lips. 'How much I love you,' he said. 'I was very jealous of you, I think you know that. Whenever you were alone with Andy...I was suspicious all the time.'

'We had several secrets,' she said, finally, thoughtfully. 'I don't think I shall have any more secrets from you, Pietro. It hurts too much. But Andy had offered to find out why my father had died. We did not know whom to suspect. Then the gems disappeared—Pietro, we were always speaking of that, not of ourselves. We never spoke any words of love between us. We never felt love, believe me,' she said earnestly, looking at him hopefully.

He squeezed her hand. 'I hope not,' he said.

'We did not. I liked him as a friend, almost like a brother. And he is going to be my brother,' she added, looking after Andy and Camilla, 'that is, if all goes well, and you approve.'

He frowned again. 'We shall see. She is very young.'

She only smiled. He would get used to the idea of the marriage of his sister and Andy. He was accustomed to thinking of Camilla as a child, and she was no longer a child.

After a pause, she finally said, against the silence of the sun-lit garden, 'Pietro, I said I would have no more secrets. But there is one more to tell you.'

He started, looking at her anxiously, his face stiffening.

'It is all right, darling,' she reassured. 'The doctor was here, you know. And he confirmed it. We are—I am—that is—we are going to have a child.'

He kept on staring at her, at her smile, at the light in her eyes, and finally his own face began to lighten, to beam. He laughed out loud, started to speak, stopped, began again.

'A child! A child! You will have my child? Yes, yes, when will it be? You are all right? You are not ill? You were ill, I was sure of it. I was afraid—'

She took his big hand in both of hers, squeezing it hard. 'Yes, I'm all right. The illness, that was normal. I shall expect the child in mid-November, I believe. Oh, I do hope it is a boy! I want the first child to be a boy!'

He was still staring, his dark eyes bright and happy and his face radiant as she had never seen it. 'A child! Oh, a child,' he whispered, and then laughed out loud again. 'Oh, it is wonderful!'

His voice was like singing as he spoke to her, his wonderful melodic voice like an Italian opera singer's she thought, smiling as he began to realize it was true.

The sunshine was warming her, the light on the garden was like a heavenly radiance blessing them. She heard Andy and Camilla laughing together, one of the women in the house was singing. Her home, she thought, her lovely radiant home in Italy, which would always be her home now. She leaned against Pietro's shoulder as he talked of the child, and knew that never in her life had she felt so secure, so loved, so safe. And should would always be safe with him, protected, secure.

279

The dark shadows hanging over her for so long had disappeared under the force of the rays of the sunshine.

She would be happy here in her golden villa, hung with yellow roses. She and her husband and her child, her family, they would all be happy here in the villa, the golden home, the Villa d'Oro.